CECE

THE END GAME

By Jaelyn Banks

Contents

Chapter 1

CECE

Denver, CO, 2018

"May I sit down?"

Timothy had been waiting for his friends at the bar for nearly twenty minutes. He noticed the woman for ten minutes, who walked over and asked to sit down. In that top and those jeans, there was no chance in hell he'd tell her no.

"I'm Timothy."

"Cece, nice to meet you."

The next half hour was filled with small talk. Although Timothy didn't find Cece's looks particularly beautiful, he couldn't help but be charmed by her confidence, approachability, and piercing eyes. But he wasn't the only person who would describe Cece that way. Nearly anyone who met her would describe her as an instantly likable person.

"I know, I know. Pushing thirty-five and still working for my father," Timothy said, straightening his coaster. Even he could hear the contempt in his voice. But that didn't seem to put this woman off.

"There's nothing wrong with a family business, as long as you can trust family," Cece replied. She was so serious and supportive. Timothy just knew this night was going to end well. Too bad he had to ruin it by asking, "And what about you, Cece? What do you do?"

Her smile grew and made him smile in return. Maybe if she finished that second cocktail, he would have the courage to get to know her on a more physical level.

Breaking eye contact, Cece began to stir her half-finished drink and said in a playful voice, "No one ever believes me when I tell them, and I don't expect you to be any different.""Well," Timothy said just as playfully, "you'll never know unless you tell me." Maybe he wouldn't need her to finish that cocktail after all.

This was working all too well. Feigning to take the bait, Cece sighed and said, "Okay. I'm a spy."

Now, it was his turn to laugh. From what he could tell, this woman was a bit clumsy and much too talkative and attention-grabbing. When she maintained eye contact this time and didn't laugh in return, his chuckle died off.

"Now, I don't know if I can believe that. You're probably telling me something ridiculous to see if I fall for it." This wouldn't be the first time a girl played that trick on him.

"No, I'm serious." Cece's mischievous smile dimmed as she said matter-of-factly, "I spy on people. Companies, mostly, but I get an occasional jealous spouse. It's not a bad gig."

Cece chose the silence that fell between them to finish her second cocktail. Studying her bar companion, she felt guilty taking advantage of his perfect room-scoping location from where she sat beside him. He looked a little bewildered.

"I still don't believe you." Timothy couldn't think of anything else to say and was flustered that she was ruining their good time.

Exhaling, she knew she had to wrap this up quickly. Her plane was going to leave in only two hours.

"Well, Timothy from Fort Collins, let me tell you a few things I've learned." Clearing her throat a little, she began, "You've had two long-term relationships in your life, and ever since the last one failed, you've decided to be more of a ladies' man than a lady's man. You like playing tennis and hiking, so you're physically fitter than you look while sitting on a bar stool. You're constantly rearranging your paper coaster, and every time I 'accidentally' bump it, you fix it to the same spot, so you're either driven by order or demand things to be your way. You're allergic to shellfish, have never broken a bone, are prone to sunburns, and have pretty good teeth for not liking the dentist." Cece paused just long enough to take a deep breath and continue.

"Your family has money, and lots of it, since you and your three siblings -two sisters and a brother, all older and in some state government position- could afford to attend a prestigious Catholic school with your childhood friend who is late showing up tonight. Your sister accidentally gave you that scar on your eyebrow last Christmas after you told them you wanted to leave the family contracting business to finish your law degree at Concord in Missouri, which is another reason you're meeting your best friend tonight. You brush it when you feel uncomfortable." Cece thought he looked rather cute when he was scared. But that wasn't all; she didn't want to leave any doubt in his mind. After all, it's rude to accuse someone of lying.

"You have a dog, but only for security purposes because you came over here straight from work instead of letting it out of your apartment on Third Avenue. That means you must have something pretty important you don't want others to get a hold of. You don't like hard liquor, but your alcohol tolerance is high since you are on your fifth beer in one hour. Working for your father's construction business wouldn't pay you enough for the high-end clothes, shoes, watch, or drinking habit you have, and there you go with your scar again."

"What the F--."

"Don't swear, I'm not done," and she wasn't.

"Your response tells me there's some foul play with the family business. It's a good thing you're leaving for Missouri. If I were in your shoes, I'd want to learn about everything I can and can't legally get away with. But whatever it is, I'm pretty sure it isn't worth the anxiety it's causing you daily."

Cece finally stopped, asked for the check, and began pulling some cash out of her wallet. "Not bad for thirty minutes, eh?"

Finishing his beer, Timothy looked like he would bolt, and she wasn't prepared to foot the bill he had racked up, too. As if she could see him replaying the evening's conversation, there was no mistaking all his responses to her questions and observations were spot on. How she got him to divulge so many personal details in such a short amount of time was both amazing and frightening. "Sh-Crap" was all he could say after the startling glare from those eyes.

Two more heartbeats passed, and Cece's smile was back on her face. "Don't worry, Timothy, I'm not here for you. Although I'll consider reaching out to your father soon, so whatever you're doing, knock it off. No, I'm here for a couple behind you. I kept stealing glances at them while you were fixing the coaster."

Timothy looked behind him and saw four middle-aged couples having a great time.

"You see the couple on the right?" Cece asked. "The wife asked me to investigate her husband. She wants to know why the restaurant he manages hires twice as many females as males and why he seems much more physically fit and pleasant despite no big changes in their marriage, income, or social status. So, if you'll excuse me, it's been a pleasure speaking with you, and I hope we never meet professionally."

Timothy was left at the bar to enjoy the rest of his night alone.

Walking over with a contagious smile, Cece exclaimed, "Hi, Mrs. Bell, I thought that was you! I'm sorry to come over unannounced, especially while you're out celebrating with friends, but I couldn't pass up this opportunity before leaving town tonight."

"Oh, Kelsie, yes." Mrs. Bell was surprised to see the woman but knew it would happen sooner or later. "I wasn't expecting to see you again so soon. It's my husband's birthday, and we're out with some of our closest friends."

"So, *this* is the husband you've told me so much about!" Cece nodded towards Mr. Bell, then, beaming at the sweet Mrs. Bell, she locked eyes with the older woman and said more deliberately, "He seems to be everything you've told me about. Again, it was nice to see you, Mrs. Bell. I hope to stay in touch."

With the message delivered, Cece walked away, knowing that two men would have very disappointing nights. Hurting sweet Mrs. Bell didn't feel very good, but this was a piggyback job, and Cece couldn't afford to get emotionally involved with her clients. After all, this was bigger than exposing one husband for getting some side action. She picked up her phone. It was time to finish her real job.

She dialed the first number while making her way through the half-crowded bar. Voicemail, good. He remembered her rule.

"Mr. Huffman, this is Cece. I will send you all the documents regarding your Denver restaurant within two hours. If you choose to take any legal action against your manager, I can get you in contact with some highly recommended attorneys. And if you know of anyone else who can benefit from my services, please pass on my contact information."

One call down, two to go. The next one was made from the back of a taxi.

"Hi Maria, this is Chelsea Markwell. There's a house I'm interested in out in Denver. It likely won't be on the market for another two months, but when it is, I suspect it will already be below market value. Put in a full offer when it's available. I'll give you the specs tomorrow."

The last call she would make was the most important, requiring complete privacy.

Chapter 2

Tulsa, OK

"Mommy!!!""Hi, sweetie, I'm back! Did you miss me?"A girl older than Chelsea remembered flew down the hall with a squeal of delight. Chelsea's daughter, Lexi, was five years old, and her sun-streaked brown hair was in pigtails. Lexi's eyes were almost a reddish brown, the carbon copy of her father's, and were ablaze with excitement over her mother's return.

Once Lexi was in her arms, Chelsea asked, "Did you miss me?"

"Yes, I did," Lexi answered. "Did you bring me anything from Colorado for my birthday?""I sure did, baby," Chelsea answered. "Here."

Producing a decorative magnet from her pocket and a wrapped snow globe from her carry-on, Lexi squealed joyfully and ran to show her new trinkets to her cousins.

"Chelsea."

She knew that tone. Her sister was the most supportive person in her life, but this trip was over Lexi's birthday, something Chelsea had promised never to do.

"Cece." This was a command to come into the kitchen.Chelsea entered the kitchen and put her suitcase on the floor and her coat on the island before responding, "Don't call me that, Miriam."

"Well, it seems to be the only name you respond to anymore. I'm the one who gave you that nickname in the first place, remember? ----I thought you would be back last week."

Oh yes, last week. Chelsea closed her eyes, knowing she had let down the two most important people in her life.

"And I did too. Please believe that. How mad was she?"

"It was her birthday—unicorn-themed. How mad do you think she was?" Miriam's anger was expected and understandable.

Chelsea had no answer. She recalled her daughter's voicemail, the birthday girl holding back sobs, saying she wished her mommy was there. It was one of two voicemails she would never delete, and both were full of heartbreak.

"Zech thinks I let you off much too easy. Saying how unfair I was when he missed Ethan's birthday last year for *his* work trip."

This brought Chelsea out of her thoughts. Pushing the pain aside regarding the other voicemail, she said emphatically, "Ha!" It was a fake laugh, but better than nothing. "I remember that. We all thought you would have a coronary."

The silence between the sisters chilled the kitchen. Miriam was getting tired of the living arrangements and freedom she gave her sister. Chelsea left every month or so, going anywhere between two days to two weeks and coming back with enough finances to live off comfortably. All Miriam knew was it had something to do with investigating people, but if she didn't have faith in her sister's strong ethics, Miriam would have guessed that it was a lie and that her sister was instead caught up in some illegal activity. Drugs, maybe. But that wasn't Chelsea. Or at least it wasn't her four years ago, but that was before Brad's passing.

While away, Miriam and Zech would watch their now five-year-old niece. Lexi was even given the home office as her semi-permanent room. It wasn't much of an inconvenience. Miriam and Zech Mullen had two children of their own, Ethan and Kayla, and the three children got along amazingly. Still, Miriam kept wondering what would happen if Chelsea ever went on a "work trip" and never returned.

That thought caused Miriam unimaginable anxiety when she heard Chelsea would extend her work trip an extra week, and she felt like she finally deserved some answers. "What are you doing, Chelsea? I know you can't tell me specifics, but what's the end game? Where is this going?"

"I have a plan, Miriam. I don't know if I can tell you yet." "But, why not! That's not fair to me, to Lexi… I need to know you're coming back next time."

Her sister's worries were valid. She had been in a few sticky spots over the last few years. That, and minimal contact with her sister and daughter during her jobs, Chelsea could easily disappear, and no one would know where to begin looking for her.

"I can't tell you what I do, Miriam, and I know that's weird, but I have an end game. I need one more big job, one more! Then, I can be done and be home full-time. I wouldn't have to go anywhere anymore."Miriam crossed her arms and tried to keep her voice even. People can control their voice and language when there are little ones nearby. "You mean because you could live off all those rental houses that keep magically popping up in your name?" she asked.

Doing her best to keep her voice even as well, Chelsea countered, "They don't magically pop up. I bought them all. I told you that." She didn't say how she got the money or how many properties she now had.

"And what then, Chelsea? After the next big job, what are you going to do?"

"Then, I'll retire and enjoy every birthday my little girl has. Not to mention my wonderful niece and nephew's birthdays. And," she said, softening her voice and facial features, "finally take the wonderful sister I love dearly on that getaway that she deserves so much."

Miriam rolled her eyes at Chelsea's childish antics and asked, "Then you'll finally tell me everything you've been doing?""Yes, Miriam. I'll tell you everything."

Miriam nodded, knowing that the answer would have to be good enough for now. But between her husband's random work trips and Chelsea's mystery business, Miriam began feeling like a single mother of three. She wondered when *she* would get that getaway they were both promising her.

Chapter 3

"Joe for my Joe!"

"Funny, Chelsea," said Joe, walking up to their favorite meeting place and accepting the hot, delicious coffee cup. "But don't think for a second a single coffee will make up for a whole lunch break. What do you need? I only have thirty minutes before I need to head back."

Joe Liebowitz was a Tulsa police officer and Chelsea's best friend. Although he was not a widower, his fate was just as sad. Days away from signing divorce papers, his still-wife had a stroke that left her needing permanent care. Being loyal to his vows, he cared for her since and still wore his wedding band. That is the type of dedication Chelsea wanted to see in every marriage, but experience told her Joe was the exception to the sad reality.

The two friends walked the same city park every time they met. It was small but had a hill to climb on the circuit, so she felt the walk wasn't a waste. It was also very public. No way was Chelsea going to let some busybody say she and Joe got a little too friendly. Never touching, they were free to converse without fear.

"I need a favor. It's been three months since my last job, and I need something. Now."

Joe looked dumbstruck. "I thought you said you were doing fine last week. What happened?"

Chelsea was a little hesitant to say. "I -- might have bought another house." Joe huffed and took a slow swig from his coffee while she continued. "I told my realtor to buy it whenever it came on the market, and it came later than expected, so I sort of forgot about it.""Are you kidding me!?" Joe loved Chelsea dearly, but he was going through a lot lately with his wife's health, and he noticed Chelsea was reaching out more for help and less just to say hi. It was putting a bit of a strain on their friendship, but he didn't want to bring that up now, and his lunch break was ending quickly."No. I wish I were kidding, but I'm not. And now I need a really big job or ten smaller ones until this mortgage is paid off." Joe shook his head in disbelief. But before he could even ask, Chelsea answered his question. "And that's it, Joe, I promise. Lexi and I will be able to be just us and live off the realty empire Brad, and I always dreamed of."

"Yeah, I know all about the dream," he said, a little too emotionless. They crested the hill but didn't make it far before Joe asked, "I know how you're getting the upper hand on all those houses, Chels. Don't you think that's double dipping a little too much?"

"You're just jealous." She retorted.

There was no reply because it was true, and they both knew it. Although he was not bitter over the hand life dealt him, it had severely hampered Joe. He was still young, only mid-thirties, and looked damn good in his cop uniform. He was also very smart funny, and never flinched when going into a dangerous situation if it meant helping someone. All in all, he was Chelsea's ideal man. But he was still married, and she was very good at separating her heart from her head.

Feeling guilty over her insensitive words, Chelsea sat on the nearest park bench and sighed. Hanging her head, she said, "I can't do my job properly in this county. Everyone knows who I am. Besides, I don't like working so close to home." Chelsea looked up at her friend, hoping he would understand this was hard on her, too. "I'm desperate, Joe."

Shaking his head, knowing he would be raked over the coals if anything went south, Joe finally sat beside her and said, "Don't worry, I think I have someone in mind. However, you might have a hard time getting the job done."

"Why, who is it?" Chelsea asked, perking up a little."Officer Tate, but not the one here, his brother out in Sapulpa. Tate's wife was a little too friendly during their last unit picnic, and he's been a tad off ever since. Even driving by his place while on shift. If he doesn't stop soon, he will likely be suspended."Chelsea nodded and said, "Females *are* harder to convict, but not impossible. I've done only one female case before."

"Really? I didn't know that."

"Yes, you did. It was one of my first ones. Remember, I had Zech play the flirt for me four years ago?""Ha! That's right. Miriam didn't talk to you for weeks after that." Zech smiled into the distance, recalling that event, and Chelsea enjoyed seeing the genuine look of happiness on his face. He didn't smile nearly as much as he should.

"I don't know why she was so mad; she knew what I needed him for." Chelsea's sarcasm was obvious, but it still earned her an incredulous look from Joe. "At least she took it better than the husband. He went ballistic, and the wife went AWOL; must have gone to live with her mom in Nevada or something." They shouldn't have chuckled over someone else's misfortune, but it couldn't be helped.

It would have felt so good to stay there, laughing over memories, but Joe's lunch break was ending, and they still needed to walk across the bottom of the hill to his car. They hadn't made it ten steps before Chelsea ruined the moment. "Unfortunately," she slowly began, "I can't use Zech again. Any chance *you* know Tate's wife?"

The walking stopped.

"No, Chels, no."

"Come on, Joe! When was the last time you were able to go on a date? And it's even a fake one."Shocked and angry, Joe murmured, "I can't do that, and you know it. I'd do anything for you, Chels, but I can't do that."

Joe briskly walked the rest of the way in silence. Chelsea followed two steps behind, mentally kicking herself for asking such a selfish question. She knew he would do anything for her, but she never should have asked such a thing of him, no matter how desperate she was.

Chelsea made it a point to apologize before he left. She lost Brad, hurt and upset; she would do anything not to lose Joe the same way. Before leaving, Joe asked what she was going to do without him. Chelse just shrugged and said, "What I always do. Take her out for too many drinks and get her to talk."

Chapter 4

Mrs. Tate had an alcohol tolerance higher than Timothy from Fort Collins. It also turned out to be an expensive waste of time. The following day, Mrs. Tate accidentally sent a dirty text message to her husband that she meant for and titled to another officer.

A speedy trial later left Chelsea with nothing more than a high drinking bill.

Joe and Chelsea were at the park again. She was practically power-walking through their meeting, with her mood as grey as the clouds threatening to pour down rain on them. Although Joe was a detective, he didn't need to be one to pick up on her irritation.

"Sorry, you missed out on that one, Chels."She sighed, knowing it was stupid to put any hope in that case in the first place. She only blamed herself. Plopping down on another park bench, Chelsea pouted, "It's okay, Joe. I wouldn't have charged for it anyway."

"Wait, what?" The confusion on Joe's face was obvious. "Why would you do that?"

Because Joe was the only person privileged to know what Chelsea did for a living, she shared everything with him after finishing her job. She always told him what her mission was, all her close calls, who was guilty and innocent… He usually asked some follow-up questions, but after all these years, he never asked *why* she did what she did before. Although she appreciated the privacy, his showing some personal interest was a nice change.

"Well," she started, "I charge differently depending on the outcome. If a wife is suspected of cheating but cleared, I only charge for my time and any resources needed to prove her innocence. But if she is guilty, let's just say I feel bad enough for the husband not to burden him more."

"But if it's the husband cheating?" Joe questioned, sitting down next to her.

"Oh, if the husband is innocent or guilty, I'm getting paid a pretty penny. But a bigger, prettier penny if he's guilty."

Joe was taken aback. "But why? Why charge for both?"Chelsea shrugged and stated, "Because the woman was either stupid enough to marry the guy or doubt him."After laughing a little, Joe asked, "Isn't that a bit sexist?"

This made Chelsea raise an argumentative eyebrow. "If a black guy calls another black guy something derogatory, is it racist?"

"No."

"Then how am I being sexist?"

Joe shook his head. This woman had some interesting ways of looking at the world. No one who knew her for a week would call her mainstream.

A quick minute passed before Joe asked, "I don't want to know how much you charge, do I?"A smirk lifted the corner of her lips. "No, Joe, you don't."

The mood was lighter now, and it would have been a great weekend get-together until three cruisers pulled into the parking lot.

Because it was the weekend, Chelsea brought Lexi with her to the park this time. Chelsea's eyes went straight to the playground in the center of the walking path. After seeing her daughter was still there, safe, and playing with a friend, she scanned the park for any possible threat. She couldn't see anything that would warrant a visit from the cops and was stunned to see the six officers heading in their direction. Joe was the first to speak.

"Sergeant Finley, is anything wrong?"

Glances were exchanged throughout the group. Sergeant Finley, however, didn't take his eyes off Chelsea. "I'm sorry, Liebowitz, but this has to do with her. Miss Markwell?"

"Sergeant Finley, you know me well enough to drop the formalities. What's going on?" Everything here screamed a red flag.

"I would like you to come with us, please.""Can you please tell me what this is about? Have I done something wrong?"

"No, ma'am," Sergeant Finley said with authority. The formalities were staying. "I'm sorry to say I can't tell you anything. But Chief Jordan requests you come, escorted, right away."

Chief Jordan. What in the world could the Chief of Police possibly want? "Joe," Chelsea asked nervously, "can you please get Lexi and bring her to the station?""Yes, but I need to leave shortly after." Joe looked a bit ashamed, and after the questioning look Chelsea gave him, he replied, "Haley has a therapy appointment."

Chelsea knew Joe's sick wife needed extra care lately, but this was the third appointment in a week. That could only mean--- her thoughts were interrupted by a sweet voice with a southern lilt. "We'll be happy to look after Lexi." It was Officer Marquis, a female officer known for her jokes and amazing Cajun food. Chelsea made it a point to make her a friend years ago and trusted her to keep an eye on Lexi at the station.Looking at the six officers and feeling all the other eyes at the park drawn to her, Chelsea agreed and called Lexi over to them. After a quick explanation to her daughter, Chelsea and Lexi were escorted to the police station, but not before nodding a silent agreement to Joe to tell him everything.

Chapter 5

Sitting alone in the Chief's office, an uneasy knot in Chelsea's stomach threatened to untangle itself in the trash bin. Chelsea reassured herself that Lexi was safe with Officer Marquis, and Joe would have been here if his wife had more reliable care, but it would have been nice to see just one supportive face right now.

Without warning, Chief Jordan walked in, proceeding to his chair without looking up from a new file. Chelsea could tell it was new because no corners had been bent from squeezing into a filing cabinet.

"Megan Paprokki, Ashley Todd, Kayla Schroder, Kayla Murray, Jessica Peoples, Emily Coy, Hailey Ped, and Jordan Chief." Chief slapped the file on the table, making Chelsea jump a little. Although Chelsea's eyes were glued to Chief, his eyes were trained on the file the entire time. "That last one made me chuckle."

An icy chill ran through her veins. He had just read eight of her last two dozen aliases. Terrified, Chelsea did her best not to falter or lose her composure.

"All known employees of the entity CECE, a private investigation company. And all of them, a one Chelsea Markwell." This is when the Chief finally looked up at her. He was very good at getting people to want to talk, and if she weren't his target of the investigation, Chelsea would have taken mental notes.

Flipping through the file, Chief fanned what was inside until pictures of her littered his desk. She is in Denver, Indianapolis, New Orleans, Kansas City, Tallahassee, and several other towns. She was caught.

"Am I in trouble, Chief Jordan?"

Strained seconds passed before he answered. "No, Mrs. Markwell, I am."

"But *why* can't you tell me where you're going this time? You've never left without at least giving me a location!" Miriam wouldn't let the issue drop ever since Chelsea told her two days ago of her newest business trip and how soon she would be leaving."I told you, sis, this is a big job. I mean, huge! And they want no leaks about the investigation.""That's never stopped you before."

She was right about that.

"Mrs. Markwell,"

"Miss."

"Miss Markwell. All signs of various heinous crimes throughout the country point to the same company, one with a branch in Tulsa. That's why I'm asking for CECE's help."

"Is this a job, or am I being blackmailed?"

"Don't insinuate foul play on my part, Miss. Markwell. I received your number from more than one source, and if you get your information within the law, there is no problem with your business. And yes, you will be paid."

That didn't quite answer her question.

"What do you need me to do?"

"Well, Chelsea? Do I get any clue as to what you're doing?""Sorry, sis." Chelsea said, and she was, "Just know this is the last one, then I promise to be home for good."

When Zech walked in, Miriam shook her head and was about to leave the living room.

"Hey honey, I'm almost set for my trip."

Miriam scoffed. "You and her both. What am I supposed to do with three kids by myself?"

This wasn't her first time, and Chelsea promised it would be her last. But as Chelsea looked closer at her sister, she saw how the strains of her job were affecting Miriam, too. When this was all over, she promised to find a way to make it up to her sister.

Zech was next to Miriam in an instant, soothingly rubbing her arms. "Honey, you know I wouldn't go unless they made me. I love being home with you and the kids."

"And I thought you were due for a promotion!" Miriam said in a huff, shrugging her arms out of his hands. "What about opening your own business like you used to talk about?"

Undeterred by his wife's reaction, Zech smiled and said, "Now, come on. I think we're doing pretty fine. Ain't that right, Chelsea?"

Zoning out over the events about to take place, there was no way for her to cover up not hearing him."I'm sorry, Zech, what?""Ah, never mind," Zech said with a wave of his hand. Pivoting, he asked, "Where are *You* off to this time?"Miriam's voice was much too clipped. "She can't say. Says it's too private for the likes of us.""Maryland!" Chelsea yelled out over her sister's answer.

Zech and Miriam turned towards Chelsea, a look of confusion on his face and irritation on hers.

"I'm going to Maryland," Chelsea said hastily. "There's a bank issue, high clearance stuff. I didn't want to tell you in case you saw me on the news."

Chelsea was a terrible liar when not in character. Her sister could see right through her and would have scolded her if not for Zech being in the room, being lied to hurt Miriam more than being left in the dark or behind. She was always stuck with the children, stuck in the everyday mundane while her husband and sister galivanted all over the country. If she couldn't know every detail of their trips, that was fine, but being lied to…there was a lot of damage needing to be repaired between sisters.

"Well, good thing we're not banking in Maryland," Zech said.

Stepping again to his stunned wife, Zech put his arms around her and pulled her close. "What do you say, honey? How about the four of us going somewhere nice as a family on my next vacation? Charleston maybe? I know you'll like it."A trip of her own did sound appealing, but until it was fulfilled, she would only see it as an empty promise. "Yeah, yeah, that would be nice," Miriam said, void of emotion.

With a kiss on her cheek, but completely unaware of the strain on his wife, Zech was off to finish packing. Chelsea was already gone when Miriam looked back towards her.

Chapter 6

Chelsea was given a file with a stack of papers to look over during her flight to Phoenix, a task that would have been easier if not squished between two strangers and stationed near the bathroom. The names and identities of one suspect and four potential accomplices were in the file.

"Your job will be simple." Chief Jordan said. "Prove he's innocent." "Innocent of what?" Chelsea asked. "Is he suspected of wasting company resources, money laundering, blackmail?" She had to bring that word back up. This was not how her job normally proceeded, and she didn't like it.

Behind the man's biography was a list of victims. Thirteen missing women over four years; ten of whom were found beaten, sexually assaulted, dead. They were all medium-build brunettes. Apart from the obvious physical features and extensive torture they went through, there was one more quality they all shared. Each was considered attractive, but not so much so that they would stand out in a crowd. In other words, pretty enough to get the attacker's attention without drawing anyone else's.

An average build, pretty brunette missing or falling victim to a heinous crime like this would not be unheard of, given half of America's female population fit that bill. The only link between them was this company and, more specifically, this company's Tulsa group and their business trips coinciding at the time of the disappearances.

"No, I can't do that. I can't spy on them, I'm sorry, but I don't do this type of job." Chelsea adamantly pushed the folder away, unable to stop shaking her head. "He's on the FBI watch list, and I need someone to clear him, give him an alibi.

Do you know how much our town will suffer if this news gets out? We can't have our town's name dragged through the mud like this."

Chelsea still had to bite back her anger at the Chief. Tulsa, not these women or their families, was his concern! But, like always, her disgust soon subsided to dread.

"And what if I can't? What if he's not innocent, or worse, gets killed by someone else while I'm on the job?"

Above the list of names and pictures was the Back Road logo. Back Road was a car rental company. Although they could not compete with the top five big names, Back Road quickly grew in popularity, focusing on smaller towns the larger companies usually overlooked.

Despite being comparatively new, they were also one of the cheaper car rental companies. They also had great frequent renter's perks.

Chelsea debated renting from them for this job. She didn't know what personal information could be accessed from a shared company database. She also didn't want any of her money funding a potentially corrupt corporation. But those frequent renter's perks.

The suspect: Cooper Gray, team leader for the most successful Back Road buying team. Under his full bio was the list of his team members and possible accomplices, with limited background information on each. They are Jonathan Thomas, Kevin President, Austin Trujillo, and Zech Mullen.

"Let's hope, for everyone's sake, he is."

Chapter 7

For renting a car, Chelsea assumed the identity of Tina Bennet, a chatty hair flipper from Maryland. *"In case Zech asked about Maryland,"* Chelsea thought. She landed in Phoenix, Arizona, a few hours before the group was planned to arrive and took the opportunity to get to the Conference Center early and check it out. The Tempe Mission Palms Hotel and Conference Center was everything they advertised. The entertainment, food, and strategic location could keep one busy for weeks, and that was without the many conferences and conventions flying through every day. Thankfully, there were many quiet places, and Chelsea soon found a place to sit and plan for the coming week.

Inside her file was the tentative "BR Boys" schedule. They were to be in town for five days, Monday to Friday and were expected to replace thirty worn vehicles with other similar models that were neither abused nor too old. That limited them to locations with fast vehicular turnover and small family lots.

The South Mountain Precinct in Phoenix and the Tempe PD recently bought new fleets and auctioned the old ones. At the same time, several family car lots in the area were on the verge of going out of business. It was a feast for vehicle vultures and, like a vulture, Chelsea expected Cooper to roam, scouring the town for cars and women.

This left Chelsea with a particularly hard assignment. Not only was she supposed to track multiple moving targets throughout the city, but she also had to hurdle the obstacle that was her brother-in-law. Her first few jobs included people she knew and blood relatives, but their roles were to help her or hire her. She had never spied on someone who could blow her cover before.

The only way she could see around the Zech problem would be to hide in plain sight. Chelsea already told Zech her job was in Maryland, so that's the lie she would feed him if they ever bumped into each other. She could picture herself telling him her "Maryland contact" sent her to watch a real estate Multi-Level Marketing team that travels to major American towns, and she is playing a Phoenix resident interested in starting her own home-renovation business or house flipping.

The faux job should be solid enough. She did that exact thing back in Washington State once, and real estate conferences happen all over the country, all the time. Surely, there will be one in Phoenix this week, right?

Chelsea wrote some hasty notes about what to do and when then moved on to the next phase: get a room.

Sitting in the lounge for a good hour before checking in, Chelsea waited for an opening with a female concierge. More specifically, the tired female concierge who kept rolling her eyes at her male colleagues when she thought no one was looking.

Approaching the counter, Cece could practically feel herself putting on someone else's skin as she donned her newest persona. She was now Tina Bennet, southern belle. She is a slightly excessive, bedazzled beauty with a thick accent to match her curly wig.

"Just leave it to a man to make the reservation!" Tina Bennet said in exasperation, putting her hand on her hip in a can't-believe-that-idiot sort of way. "I'm the newest member of the Back Road crew," Tina shook her keys to show the Back Road keyring. She added, "But you would think after the last time we had a work trip, they would remember to get me my room!"Shocked by the sudden appearance before her, the concierge shook her head slightly to clear it and respectfully asked, "I'm sorry Mrs…?""Miss Bennet," Chelsea said, emphasizing the "miss." The thin, white line where her wedding ring once sat was still on her finger, as she had only removed it last year, but if she was going to make this painful step forward, the least people could do was call her Miss again. "Miss Bennet. I apologize for the inconvenience." With that, the woman plastered on an ever-so-practiced smile. "Let's see what we can do to fix this."

After giving the names of her "coworkers" and throwing in some low-key male criticism, Tina Bennet had a friend at the hotel in under three minutes. She didn't expect to get into any sticky spots this time, but having at least one hotel staff member on her was always a good idea—especially one with access to room numbers.

"The closest room we can put you in is on the same side of the conference center, but down a floor. Would that be sufficient?" Afterward, the concierge gave her the Back Road Boys room number and detailed three ways she could get from her hotel room to theirs.

With a flick of her wrist, Miss Bennet answered, "What a peach you've been, thank you! And since I'll get reimbursed anyway, can I pay with my credit card? Those points add up, and I sure could use a trip somewhere alone!"The woman behind the counter smiled and said, "Yes, Miss Bennet, we require payment upfront anyway. That will be $267.45."With a comically skeptical look, Miss Bennet chuckled and said, "For four nights? Goodness me, whatever hotel promotion my company goes through, sign me up!" "No, Miss Bennet," the woman said, her smile faltering, "your group is booked for only one night."

Alarms blared in Chelsea's mind, but Miss Bennet didn't skip a beat. Doing a perfect hair toss to recover, she laughed a little at herself and did what she does best: lied. "Oh, that's right, it's Nashville where we're staying four nights. Honestly, honey, maybe it *is* a good thing I'm not making the reservations."

Leaving the concierge fully convinced by her ditzy performance, Tina Bennet took her room key and nearly jogged to her room. Her normal jobs gave her a feeling of confidence, or at least a mini power-high, but ever since Chelsea heard the details pertaining to this one, her stomach was in a constant state of queasiness.

Chelsea never had an easily upset stomach until she had Lexi. However, it was not brought on by food or other physical indulgences, like most other moms, but rather through emotional upheaval. More specifically, Chelsea threw up when she felt afraid or overly anxious.

Was it an inconvenience? Most definitely. On the other hand, it taught Chelsea how to calm her emotional state, which proved to be a tremendous help over the last four years. Also, not wanting the stomach acid to ruin her smile, she kept her on a strict dental schedule.

Chelsea felt back on her game after a quick face rinse and deep breathing to calm her stomach. Good thing. It was time to get to work.

Chapter 8

It was after eight, and Chelsea was starving. She had missed dinner, a problem she hoped would soon be remedied. Factoring in her target's airport arrival time, traffic, car rental time, and possibly a quick bite on the road, the BR Boys would be arriving at the hotel any moment, as she had nicknamed them. Wig gone and dressed to kill, Chelsea hoped this gamble would pay off. She sat down again in the lobby, faced the doors, and waited.

Cooper was the first through the door. Being the pack's leader, it wasn't surprising to see him with nothing but his unnecessarily large wallet in hand. The short bio in Chelsea's file labeled him assertive, full of bravado, and possessing a sense of self-eminence. He was in his late thirties, quite good-looking, and thankfully single. Not just because she couldn't picture a woman ever putting up with such a man, but the best way for him to showcase his dominance around his co-workers was to get the girl. Acting like a ditzy, borderline slut was her ticket in.

Kevin and Austin were next through the door, with most luggage. Both are married, both mid-forties, and both are well educated. Chelsea figured they were there for one of three reasons. They were either unaware of their potential, sick of being with their wives and liked a job that allowed plenty of traveling opportunities, or, with a darker thought, were a part of the sinister things at play.

She observed them closely, trying to gauge their personalities as they interacted with the front desk staff. They were tired, but even while burdened with the bulk of the luggage, they were still cordial with the person behind the desk. Chelsea might see them enjoying some time away from home and family responsibility, but she didn't consider them sinister.

That made sense. They were people pleasers. Their age, physical qualities and years of being demanded by spouses and offspring made them personable, and their job was to make first contact with the company. Once their kind, patient, gentle demeanor opened a door, it was up to one of the other three to seal any deals.

Although the phrase, "you catch more flies with honey than vinegar," was never one of her favorites, Chelsea could tell that's exactly what they did. They were the honey designed to attract flies to Cooper's cut-throat vinegar.

Chelsea didn't see Jonathan enter the hotel, but he was soon standing behind Kevin and Austin, talking on the phone with either his fiancé or one of tomorrow's appointments. He was the planner, as well as their techie. Methodical to a fault, Chelsea wouldn't be surprised if a spreadsheet on his computer organized which shirt would be worn any given day of the month. He was no nerd, though. The file labeled him as quite the daredevil, and his social media presence confirmed it.

Chelsea knew there was more to each man than the file provided. Labeling someone as a daredevil without specifics was also foolish. With too broad a spectrum, for all Chelsea knew, his hobbies fell from ax throwing to regularly donating his body to science as a guinea pig.

Thankfully, a quick media search via conference center Wi-Fi brought up many pictures, mostly consisting of outdoor activities. Skiing, sky diving, white water rafting, swimming with sharks, and many other adventures were plastered all over the internet.

Other than risking his life regularly for fun's sake, something about Jonathan seemed off. Jonathan was publicly engaged, so why were there so many pictures of him out and about on crazy adventures and none of his fiancée? There could be a reasonable explanation, like them having a shared media account dedicated to their relationship and joint adventures, but Chelsea was pretty good at finding people. His fiancée was nowhere. This didn't sit well with Chelsea.

Zech was meandering into the hotel, a few minutes behind the rest. He was also on the phone like Jonathan, but if Chelsea had to guess, it was with Miriam. Chelsea stepped out of her concealed vantage point to a spot the other BR Boys couldn't see and did her best to wave Zech down covertly. It was obvious the moment he noticed her. With eyes widening like a deer in the headlights, Chelsea could have sworn he went a shade paler. It was not quite the response she hoped for, but it could be explained by the fact that she *was* supposed to be on the other side of the country—that, or the scandalous outfit she was wearing.

Putting her finger to her lips, she held up her other hand like a phone, shook her head, and mouthed "no."

"Hey, Honey, I got to go. Kiss everyone for me… Okay, I love you too, bye." Good, he didn't tell Miriam.

While waiting in her room, after the bombshell of knowing the Back Road Boys were only staying one night, Chelsea decided to tweak her approach. Zech needed to help her again. Ditching the wig but still putting on her Tina persona, she slinked up to her brother-in-law in a seductive way that would have otherwise been considered comical or damnation-worthy.

"Hey stranger, looks like you and I are working the same conference center.""Chelsea, what the hell are you doing here?" Zech demanded in a harsh whisper. "And why are you dressed like that?""First, it's Tina Bennet," Chelsea said in her once again thick accent."What?"

Obviously, he wasn't following along, so Chelsea gave him a little help. Dropping the accent, Chelsea pretended to brush some imaginary dust off his shoulder and quietly said, "If you *ever* talk to me, you need to get the name right. Got it? Second, Maryland sent me this way to investigate a real estate Multi-Level Marketing scam. I'm playing the local, hopeful home flipper, and yes, Miss Bennet will be a bit of an attention-grabbing ditz. P*lease* don't let your co-workers or Miriam know because I can't lose this job, Zech. This is my last big one, and then I can get out, go home, and be free."

"If you're working a real estate MLM conference, why are you talking to *me*?" This was more of a demand than a question. And he had a good point. It's a good thing she already had a good answer."Well, that's because the guy I need to watch happens to be a complete alpha male. If he sees me with another guy, he'll do practically anything to talk with me in private. Sorry, but I'm using you as bait.""Damn it, Chel…whatever your name is.""Tina Bennet.""I don't care, I don't want to know, and I don't want to help. I can*not* be sucked into this right now. I have…oh crap."

Zech looked up to see Cooper coming towards them. Chelsea felt guilty playing Zech over, but this was the make-it or break-it point, and this case was bigger than his feelings. Before Cooper made it over to them, Chelsea leaned in toward Zech in a way in-laws should never do and whispered, "Fine, you don't want to be my bait. I'll get someone who will," then a little louder, "Oh, I'm so sorry Sugar. I thought you were someone else."

Obviously, her actions put Zech in an uncomfortable position, but with Cooper so near, all he could do was play along whether he liked it or not. "Well, Tina, it was nice to meet you. I hope you find what you're looking for."

Hoping he heard her silent prayer of thanks, she gave him a large, flirty smile and said, "Oh, I'm sure I'll find who I'm looking for soon enough. Have a good night, Mr. Mullen, was it?" She waited just until Cooper was close enough to see her wink goodbye and walk away towards the hotel's bar. She knew she had the single man's attention. Now, all she had to do was make sure she kept it.

Chapter 9

Seven minutes was all she had to wait. Not even asking to sit down, Cooper grabbed the bar stool next to her and leaned in with manly suaveness meant to impress her. Tina would play right into it, making her inner Chelsea cringe. "It was Tina, right? I noticed you talking with Mr. Mullen. I'm Cooper Gray, his team leader.""Tina Bennet," she replied. "Don't tell me you're another good-looking, but unfortunately for me, happily married man too.""Oh no, I am most definitely not."

Cooper didn't break eye contact with her the whole time. He edged slowly toward her until he was close enough to trail a finger up and down her forearm. This made Chelsea finish her drink a little sooner than she wanted.

Getting the wrong idea, Cooper asked, "What are you drinking?""Depends, are you buying?"Finally taking his finger off her arm, Cooper leaned back to showcase his physique and, in a tone one would usually use when they were challenged, asked, "Would I have asked if I wasn't?"

Man, this guy was good at getting what he wanted. Chelsea made a show of giving him a body check before giving him her drink order and putting on the performance of her life. After all, it's not easy playing a player—especially one you would never want.

Chelsea did her best spying while Cooper ordered drinks. A lot about a person is communicated without saying a thing. Although words and tone are important, Chelsea looked for details to see beyond the obvious.

The first thing she noticed was Cooper walked into the hotel with a strut, but his gait was tighter, more of a limp, when he walked into the bar. What could have happened between then and now to change how he walks? Was this man naturally clumsy but put on a charade much like she does when wanting to get someone's attention?

The second thing she noticed was his smell. It was stronger now than in the lobby, and he smelt good. Guys like him who smell *that* good know it and use it to their advantage, getting the response they want despite their horrible personality.

The third thing she noticed was his clothing. He had changed, not just into a clean shirt, but one in a color that enhanced his natural features.

The fourth thing she noticed was his watch, wallet, and shoes. His watch was a sleek, modern timepiece and probably had features he didn't know about. His wallet was either new or barely used, but since this was now the second time she had seen it in only ten minutes, she would go with her first guess. Chelsea could tell it was high-quality leather without even needing a close look. His shoes were similar. Giving off that new, polished vibe, his shoes matched his outfit and suggested he had pairs that matched every outfit he owned.

What did all these tell Chelsea? It advised her he was calculated. It told her he was prepared. It told her he was extremely vain. It told her he was somehow bringing in more money than Back Road should be paying him. But louder than all those, it told her that, for Cooper to have perfected this game, he must have been playing it for a *long* time. After all, practice makes perfect.

Three drinks in, and Cooper was happily talking about himself non-stop. This led Chelsea to a cornucopia of privileged information.

Normally, it took some persuasion to get people talking about themselves, but all it took was some basic praise for doing his minimal job requirements or commenting on how his co-workers were beneath him. Only after Cooper recited the long list of places he had recently traveled to (some of which she was all too familiar with thanks to the file upstairs on her bed) was he finally ready to turn the conversation to her.

"You know, Tina, you are exactly what I hoped to find in Arizona."Knowing he was not, and likely never would be, the kind of guy she would go for, Chelsea hid her disdain well. Giggling a little too brightly and giving a playful shoulder push, Tina began to reel him in. "Oh, don't go saying that. Coming from a guy like you, I might get the wrong idea. Besides, you probably find what you're looking for everywhere you go."Cooper smiled the perfect half-smile before stating, "I might, but I'm here now, aren't I? By the way, what brings you to town, and how long are you here for?"Chelsea inwardly rolled her eyes. It was about time he asked something about her. "Oh, I live on the Phoenix metro's far side. I'm just staying here because I didn't want to deal with the traffic every morning." Leaning in closer than necessary, Chelsea accidentally brushed herself against him. She whispered in a voice only he could hear, "I'm going to start my own real estate empire, and the conference here is going to help make me rich."Chelsea was pretty sure he didn't hear anything other than the word "rich," but after her body accidentally bumped up against him, she wasn't sure he needed to hear anything at all. Leaning away again, Chelsea was ready to end the night and get away to write down what she knew. "Thank you for the drinks, Cooper. Maybe I'll see you again before you leave town?"Cooper seemed a little let-down hearing that. "You're leaving already? It's still early. And since you're a local, I figured you could show me around the place."

His mind was focused on her showing him something other than the town, and she knew it. She expected this to happen and inwardly praised herself for thinking ahead, paying off the bartender before Cooper arrived to dilute her drinks. The bartender made a killer tip, and she didn't go to bed with a suspected killer. It was a win-win."I like how you think, Cooper. However, I've been warned beauty and brains are deadly."He gave his signature smile and, looking her over for not the first time that night, said, "Just wait and see."

Man, he was such a creep. But Chelsea couldn't let her personal feelings get in the way. Wanting her to get drunk enough to get lucky, or at least not fight when he got a little too handsy, Cooper seemed a little agitated about her not being more intoxicated. Knowing his type, he would likely set his eyes on someone easier. She couldn't allow that, but she drew a blank on her next move for the first time in forever. Thank goodness, she didn't have to come up with anything too crazy.

"Hey, Cooper! We got a call from corporate in five. We need you upstairs."It was Zech who saved the night. Thank God for her brother-in-law."Seriously, man! Can't you see I'm off the clock?"Anger could be justified in such a situation, but Cooper was more than just a little angry. Knowing there probably wasn't a conference call, Chelsea didn't want to see Zech get in trouble over her."Cooper, I have an idea." Saying his name drew him back to her. Strategically placing her hand on his thigh, she waited until she was the only thing in the room he saw. "How about you tell me what your plans are for tomorrow, and I'll make sure to run into you? Give you that tour of the town you've been asking for."

Cooper glanced over at Zech, who promptly got the message to go away. "Make it quick, Cooper. Four minutes."And just like that, Chelsea got everything she needed: Cooper's whereabouts tomorrow and a way out of tonight.

Chapter 10

Chelsea never slept well the first few nights of a new job, and since her jobs were wrapped up on an average of eight days, she rarely slept well on a job, period. Last night was no exception. Images of Valley Girls alive one minute and dead the next haunted her for the three hours she was asleep.

After the sun finally peaked over the horizon, Chelsea was more than ready to end this job.

Looking through the file last night, Chelsea knew there were two cars allotted to the group during jobs, which Chelsea would have tagged in the parking lot if she knew which ones they were. Waiting for them in the lobby, with her notepad in hand and donning a non-descript outfit, Chelsea watched all five men leave at the same time. Cooper and Kevin took one midsize car to, if he were truthful to her last night, the South Mountain Precinct auto auction while Austin, Jonathan, and Zech took another midsized car to, Chelsea would have assumed, tackle a nearby car lot that was on their to-do list. However, she knew that was only partly true.

It pricked her conscience a little to do this, but Chelsea knew her brother-in-law's email password. After all, who else was she supposed to practice her spy skills on but those closest to her and quickest to forgive her trespasses?

Since she couldn't sleep anyway, Chelsea waited until most individuals would be asleep and snuck into Zech's email. She wrote down a detailed itinerary to replace the tentative one Chief gave her and some other tidbits from back-and-forth co-worker emails. And to guarantee no trail led directly back to her, she did it all with her trusty pencil and paper pad.

The first red flag Chelsea saw was their itinerary. Unless this team was quite inept, there was no way they needed a whole week to visit two precincts, three car lots, and one auction house. Especially if they had two vehicles and could split up. However, Chelsea didn't know how these dealings were done, and maybe it *did* take all day to buy cars.

The second flag was much more startling.

According to her notes, Jonathan scheduled a vacation day to hike around South Mountain. He must plan to drop off the other two on his way out of town. But Chelsea just saw him leave the conference center, and unless Jonathan was wearing hiking clothes fit for the Arizona desert under his nice slacks and polo, that was an obvious lie.

Chelsea planned on following Cooper, but once she saw Jonathan striding in through the lobby, she made him the only one on her radar. She couldn't afford to have anyone unaccounted for, at least for now.

Chelsea had been following Jonathan for nearly an hour. For someone who was considered to be so organized, Jonathan seemed to be rather clumsy when navigating. Snaking through the city and backtracking more times than she cared for, Chelsea found it difficult to follow such a nondescript car. However, she eventually tailed him to a neighborhood southeast of South Mountain. Trying not to follow too closely but still being able to identify which car was his, Chelsea saw Jonathan stopped at a house that backed against the mountainous park. Googling the address, it looked like a decent-sized Airbnb.

It was much cheaper than the conference they were currently staying at. If one privately rented the house but turned in reimbursement papers for the conference center, each person could pocket quite a bit of money over the year. It also allowed all of them their room. If anything, this was the way to travel with such a large group.

This also was a relief for Chelsea. If Cooper or any combination of these guys were responsible for the list of murders on her passenger seat, they would need privacy and a confined space, and a house like this wouldn't provide either. Were these guys illegally lying to their company and cheating on hotel reimbursement? Yes, definitely. But did this justify being on the FBI watch list? It was still too early to answer that.

Not wanting to turn in her sister's husband over something so trivial as a few hundred bucks here and there, Chelsea drove away before any other incriminating evidence could be found.

Chelsea made it back to the conference center long before she originally expected. This gave her ample time to gather her things and review what she thought about the case.

Cooper, although a creep, seemed much too open about himself and what he liked in women. And he showed no reaction when she casually threw around a few victims' first names disguised as fake friends. From what she gathered, he was a cocky, touchy jerk, not a serial killer. This case, as far as she was concerned, was closed.

Calling the Chief and leaving a voicemail, "Good, he remembered not to pick up." Chelsea gave her opinion and said she was finished and heading home that evening.

Emailing her report from the downstairs complimentary computers and checking out at the concierge, Chelsea didn't expect to see Cooper behind her when she turned to leave, startling the breath out of her.

"Are you going somewhere?" Cooper eyed the bags, more than needed for "living" across town. "Oh, hey, you! I *would* stay here the whole conference, but I couldn't sleep on that darn mattress. Also, I left my phone charger at home, so I thought I might as well stay since I'm forced to go there anyway."Instantly distracted from the luggage, Cooper donned his perfected, smug smile and, taking a step closer, practically cooed, "Well, if it's a comfy bed you're looking for, I have one at my new place. Grab your charger and meet me there. I have an afternoon appointment, but I'll be done around seven. We can grab something to eat, and I can tuck you in for the night. What do you say?""Eww" was what she wanted to say. And what the heck, she had all she needed; she might as well have a little fun messing with him before she left town. Playing it up, Chelsea smiled back and countered, "How about you give me the address, and I'll have a surprise waiting for you when you get there?"His full smile told her she had a deal. "4018 E Western Star Boulevard"

During a brief pause, Chelsea's smile only faltered for a millisecond, but a million sirens blared in her ears in that short time. "What?" "Do you want me to write it down? Here." Cooper grabbed the nearest paper and began writing his number and the address. "No, no, I heard you. I didn't expect that street."The chuckle he gave while he finished writing the location down didn't indicate whether he was confused or if he found her answer genuinely funny. Keeping a tight hold on the note when Chelsea reached for it, his teasing smile made her feel nothing but queasy. "Why? Exactly what were you expecting?" When she didn't answer, he let go of the note. What was she expecting? The truth? Not that. That wasn't the address she followed Jonathan to.

"I'll see you around seven."

Chapter 11

If Chelsea had made a list of her feelings sitting on the cool floor after a violent episode in the nearest conference toilet, she would have written down words like blind-sided, stupid, mad, sick, and scared. Yes, those would have made the top of a long list. Those feelings were too much for Chelsea to come down from, and her poor stomach and any other guests who were witnesses were punished for it.

Chelsea broke the first rule of being CECE: no emotional attachments and she spent a good twenty minutes in that bathroom stall beating herself up over it.

In her desperate hope to find Cooper innocent: for the Chief's sake, for Zech's sake, for Tulsa's sake, as well as her own (because she did not need the knowledge of purposefully going on a date with a serial killer on her conscience), Chelsea looked back and saw how she mentally excused some questionable actions.

What business team schedules to be gone for a week only to complete most of their requirements in one day? What business team rents a high price hotel for one night, then turns around and stays in an average house? Okay, money was involved in that one, but for all anybody knew, they were still at the conference center. They were off the radar at the house and free to do as they pleased. And the communal house she followed Jonathan to was not just any house. It backed up to a park with many trails to get lost in.

Her job was far from over. Dialing the Chief's number again, her hand froze above the call button.

She remembered how haggard her sister looked, how much Zech enjoyed his trips, and what this news would do to both.

She thought about how this job was supposed to put an end to all her traveling and spying, but now it had turned into this ugly, disgusting hunt for a serial killer. That last thought made Chelsea wish she wasn't so hasty in leaving the restroom. She really, *really* could have just had a date with a serial killer.

Flashes flew through her mind when she sat on a nearby couch with her head in her hands. Picture after picture of victims, reports, and images of a man who ruined so many lives made her hold back more than one gag. Above all the images and thoughts vying for her attention, there was one conversation she couldn't drown out.

"And what if I can't clear him? What if he's not innocent?" "Let's hope, for the sake of everyone involved, he is." "But what if I CAN'T?"….. "Then prove he's guilty."

Chelsea never made that call to Chief. It was risky, staying behind when the only other person who knew where she was thought she would be home in a few short hours. Part of her wanted to believe it was due to bravery, keeping her mission a secret, even from the one who hired her, but deep down, she knew it was shame. Tucking your tail between your legs and admitting you were wrong is hard. She just told Chief Cooper was, well, not innocent, but not deadly. If she was going to contradict herself, she either needed a pile of proof or to tell Chief face to face.

Chapter 12

On top of sleep deprivation, time was never on Chelsea's side when she had a job. Usually, it was her employer's deadline, but rarely was it the suspect's. Chelsea knew the Back Road Boys were only staying five days and four nights in Arizona. That left less than four days and three nights to wrap up the biggest job of her spy "career."

Rushing through the aisles of the nearest hardware store, Chelsea did some shopping. There were certain gadgets she never went on a job without her favorite tracking devices, microphones, versatile shoes, and a variety of disguises. Yet, when it came to bugging two houses at once—with not just ears, but eyes too— in Arizona, Chelsea lacked two more necessities: Duct tape and some good hiking boots.

After googling the address Cooper gave her, Chelsea felt queasy again. It was exactly the kind of house to host the suspected crimes. It was in the old part of town where there was more side yard, and thus more space to operate and more distance from prying neighbors. To add points to its creep factor, the house also backed up to three major South Mountain hiking trails. This was a blessing in disguise, providing not just a perfect place to hide someone but, in her case, for someone to hide.

The only cashier was a tad slow at his task, but that gave Chelsea more time to think over her task. Chelsea only realized there were a few more items she should pick up before leaving the store when she was next in line. When she returned to the same cashier, Chelsea now had a second roll of duct tape, a cheap funnel, a black light, tweezers, and excessive chewing gum.

"Looks like you're going to have an interesting night."

The older man's comment caught Chelsea off guard at first, but then she saw the twinkle in his eyes. He was making fun of her random purchases. She should have kept her mouth shut, but cashiers rarely have genuine conversations with their customers these days, and Chelsea was not going to miss this opportunity to speak with a stranger, especially if she could mess with them a little.

Picking up a roll of duct take and the tweezers, Chelsea said, "Yep! I found my guy cheating on me the other day, and I plan on using these babies to get a full confession."

The older man did look taken aback, but Chelsea wasn't done. "The new shoes and black light ensure I don't miss anything in the clean-up. And if I'm now chewing something, my mouth gets too dry."

With his brow furled but unable to stop himself, the older man asked, "And the funnel?"

Chelsea smiled before answering. "That one's a surprise."

Taking the receipt offered to her, Chelsea left, taking her bags with her. Glancing towards the security camera screens, Chelsea saw the cashier's eyes were fixed on her retreating figure, completely ignoring the other customer waiting to be checked out. She had to make sure not to laugh within the cashier's hearing range.

Chapter 13

There were only 3 hours left before Chelsea met Cooper, and she had a lot to do. She had only put eyes and ears on one other house before this job, and there was a lot of trial and error. There is no way to run a continuous video circuit without the camera being hooked to an electrical source. However, a motion-activated trail camera doesn't have that issue.

Walking up the street to Cooper's address, Chelsea couldn't tell if this neighborhood had zero crime, was completely abandoned, was filled with hermits, or consisted of owners who all had day jobs. Either way, Chelsea saw no home security signs or outside cameras, so she hid one trail camera on a neighbor's scraggly tree and zoomed in on the front door of Cooper's place. She wouldn't get more than a time stamp and a general picture of whoever went in and out of the place, but it was still photo evidence that could be accepted in court. Having notifications sent to her phone when a picture was taken also told her if the place was empty.

Going around the back, Chelsea found an old window that wasn't shut all the way and forced it open. Chief was very adamant about not breaking the law, but she felt getting arrested to save another woman's life was worth the risk. Besides, it's not like she had never broken the law before… Not flinching, Chelsea entered the premises and put ears on the place.

Walkie-talkies are underrated. Sure, the sound quality is only good if you're practically eating the microphone, and they are nowhere near the bugs she planned on using at the Big House. Still, if you're in a pinch and need to listen in on a private conversation at a relatively safe distance, a few ten-dollar packs of walkie-talkies will do the trick. That is, as long as no one whispered and no one else was around on the same frequency.

While still in the car, Chelsea opened two four-packs of long-range walkie-talkies, muted all but one, and set the others to different channels. Duct-taping the transmitter buttons down would cut their battery life to less than one day, but it was the best she could do. She only had three days left anyway.

Pulling one from a shopping bag, it was quickly placed in the only bedroom, on the part of the wall just above the inside of the closet door. Thankfully, the house was *not* updated, and the closet had an accordion door. When testing the audio, she could hear all over the room. The second went on top of the fridge, pushed out of reach, and a third was taped behind the couch. Number four was taped securely to the underside of a dining room chair to pick up conversations around the small dining room table, and number five was behind a post in the garage, just in case. Chelsea didn't like taping one under a chair that could be picked up, knocked over, or loosened if sat on too hard…but options were limited, and dang it, she was going to get her money's worth out of these things.

Satisfied with her work, she slipped back through the window, but instead of going back to the front of the house, she walked straight onto one of the trails the house backed up to. She followed it about a quarter of a mile to another street where her Back Road car awaited her: one house down, one to go.

Chapter 14

Two things made eavesdropping on the bigger house more than twice as difficult as the tiny house. It was easily three times bigger than Cooper's tiny house and already occupied by the Back Road Boys. She debated with herself the best way to at least get ears on the place but sidestepped to tag the cars while she contemplated quickly. Unfortunately, there was only one in the driveway.

Realizing why, Chelsea whispered, "Crap." She had lost track of time.Looking at her watch, it was about ten to seven. Cooper must have taken the second car to their non-existent date. Guess he was going to get a surprise after all.

Her phone must have been on vibrate because she didn't hear the front door trail-cam notification go off. Being only two miles apart, she would be given no more than a four-minutes warning if someone was traveling between houses, and if she were anywhere in the vicinity, she would need every second of it.

But her phone wasn't on vibrate. Cooper never went to the Tiny House. That was odd, but there was still a lot of work to do, and she couldn't waste time dwelling on it. Ensuring her volume was turned up so she didn't miss when Cooper finally made an appearance, Chelsea parked three houses up the street and grabbed a car tracker, three high-tech bugs, a black light, and a funnel.

To Chelsea, tracking cars was easy. It might be over-done in the movies or mystery books, but the tie-the-shoe trick worked every time. She even undid her bootlaces to make that bit real so as not to draw suspicion. After her newly purchased, heavy-duty hiking boots were tightly laced up, and a tracker was secured in the wheel well of a Back Road car, she continued down the street to another trail access point. Sneaking up the front porch would have been the easiest approach, but with the insubstantial vegetation, coverage was iffy at best, and these neighbors were much more out and about. Chelsea could not afford to be seen or, worse, questioned.

The evening trails were busier than she wanted, but that was another inconvenient blessing. Passing three couples in the distance to the house, her fear of snakes subsided. Chelsea knew, from other jobs in desert towns, to be aware of the three big outdoor dangers: snakes, scorpions, and spiders. The other two are not as skittish by foot traffic.

From counting rooftops, Chelsea's experience from past jobs came in handy once again. Needing to painfully get through about twenty yards of desert shrubs and other less pleasant vegetation, her heavy boots did manageable work through the cacti and sagebrush. Her jean-clad legs, however, were scratched and poked at, protected but not entirely against their prickly assaults.

The backyard could barely be called that, not that Chelsea's pincushion legs were complaining. A split-rail fence and an arm's length of manicured lawn separated the back porch from the thorns and thicket. Nearly hugging a shade tree that covered most of that distance, Chelsea could easily reach the back of the house.

The pale sunset had almost faded into an indigo night, and with darkness comes danger. Withdrawing her black light, Chelsea checked the house's exterior for any stinging friends. Good thing there was a scorpion not too far from her right foot. Swallowing her anxiety, she was thankful the window she needed was to her left.

Zech was the type of person who always cracked a window rather than running the air conditioner or heater. He also didn't seem affected as much as a normal person by temperature change. Knowing that, a cracked back window letting in the quickly cooling night air was not a huge plus, and it rendered the funnel she brought useless, "for now," she thought. Ever since she saw her nephew listen in on a private conversation by putting a funnel to the room's window, she had wanted to try it out on the field. Maybe next time.

Her disappointment didn't last when creeping silently closer. The conversation inside drifted to her ears. She was unsure whose voice was whose, but that mattered little compared to the content. She could tell by some slight slurring that these men were having more than a few drinks, and that meant the conversation topic was not carefully guarded.

"Oh man, you guys should have seen her. I would have devoured her all night if she gave the word.""Yeah? Well, I was there too, Kevin, and you can have her. Our pool happens to have fish in it, not bottom dwellers." Hollers of sick humor roared in her ears while someone else tried to defend the man. If she could concentrate for a second, she could decipher who was who, but they didn't slow down enough to let her."Now, hold on there. I've seen that fiancé of yours, Jonny, and bottom dwellers or not, at least the women we're attracted to are good enough to take pictures of."An angry voice flared back at him, "Shut up! Give me ten seconds with your face and see how much action you'll get when I'm done!""Whoa, he's right, Austin, that's going too far." That voice she recognized. Zech. "Oh, sure. Coming from Mr. Celibate over here. When will you get off your high horse and have a little fun? Cooper got another place not too far from here. We'll hold the phone and cover for you if the wifey feels like calling again.""Yeah, what will that be, Zech, the tenth one today?""Hey, trust me, guys, I have two very good reasons for not chasing after these girls you call women. One, I get so much action. If I kept track, I'd have more notches than you three put together."

This statement drew doubtful balks from the other men. Chelsea didn't need to know all about her sister's marriage, but if it kept him from sleeping around, good for her. Trying to shout above the protests, Zech finally got out, "And two! Miriam is also pretty enough to take pictures of."More rounds of laughter with only one voice objecting filled the air.

Chelsea had done this enough to know that idle talk of drunk guys was often a goldmine of information. Cooper was not the only one using the tiny house, but he was very much in control. They even called it Cooper's house. This meant her suspect list significantly increased, but Cooper remained her prime suspect. Chelsea could also have photographic evidence that would warrant two more divorce jobs. Even if she wasn't proud of it, she was saving these wives from some real douche bags. Thank goodness Zech wasn't one of them. If she had to break that kind of news to Miriam…the thought alone began to make her queasy.

Taking as much conversation as she could stomach, Chelsea prayed while applying some adhesive to the back of a bug. She carefully reached up with a black-gloved hand to gently press it against the lower window pane. The boys were too caught up in each other's egos and various recounting of rendezvous with women to notice. The bug was much more efficient than a walkie-talkie and should stay charged the entire trip. And for as long as Zech was at the house, the window should remain open.

Consulting the black light again, it looked to Chelsea like the scorpion wasn't going anywhere soon. Gathering her courage, she skirted around the critter towards the other end of the house where the bedrooms supposedly were. She checked all the windows she could reach, and only one was unlocked: a thankfully oversized bedroom window where the bed was blessedly below the windowsill.

Chelsea didn't consider herself the athletic type, and crawling into an occupied residence through the window was not something she could ever see doing before now. Chances were, she would make a lot of noise trying to get in, even with the oversized window.

She stuck an earbud into her ear that was connected to the bug she just planted near the guys. She waited until the next inappropriate comment for the perfect laughter cover, allowing her to shimmy the window up enough to get through. Good thing, too, because it stuck a little and squeaked. Waiting again for laughter to cover the unfortunate grunts involved in climbing through a window, she sent up a silent prayer of thanks for the bed under her to buffer her fall. At least that didn't squeak.

Chelsea didn't even realize she was holding her breath until another round of laughter rang through her ears. The room was small and had minimal furnishings. Recognizing the bag on the floor and some clothes sticking out proved this was Zech's room. That made sense. The window was unlocked.

Checking her footing with every step, she slid towards the door. The Back Road Boys were unaware of her presence, and enjoying a little story, Jonathan was retelling about an adventure he had in Connecticut a few months ago. A slight peek under the door told her this bedroom was in full view of the dining room where the men sat. It was too risky to plant ears anywhere out there now, and she still didn't know if or when Cooper would be back.

While she was still on the floor, Chelsea put a bug just behind the dresser next to the door. She would have chosen a better location if she could get out of the room or if the bedroom was any bigger. But she couldn't; it was the closest she could get to a hall bug for now. As a bonus, if anyone randomly moved the dresser away from the wall, it would look like a piece of trash or a dead bug on the ground. She didn't like bugging Zech's room.

Chelsea was kneeling and about to get up when her phone notification went off. Freezing, she heard the worst thing possible in her ear. "Hey, what was that?" "Did it come from the hall?" "Wasn't mine." "My phone's right here." "Did Cooper say he was leaving his phone again?"

The time for being quiet was over. Grabbing as many nearby items as she could, Chelsea scrambled to the window and practically leaped out, taking a corner of the blanket with her. Depositing the items on the ground as a distraction, she ran, praying for at least thirty seconds to get down the street and to her car. She didn't drive away but sat in the back seat, hoping the stationary car would be perceived as vacant.

She remained there, her earpiece glued to her ear, until the voices on the other end confirmed the coast was clear. They believed it was a botched robbery. Shakily making her way to the front seat, her pulse was through the roof, and the only thing she could think was, "Omigod, omigod, omigod," as she made her way to the nearest gas station.

She verbally scolded herself. Did she not purposefully turn the volume up on her phone? Was she so stupid as to not check the only thing that could give away her presence *before* entering the house!? She never messed up, never! But then again, she was doing a lot of firsts this trip.

This was her first time breaking into a house she wasn't previously invited in to. This was also her first time doing a job where she knew someone involved. And this was her first time being blackmailed, or at least feeling that way, into the job in the first place. She particularly hated that last one. And with two of her five days now finished, she was sure many more firsts would occur.

Then she remembered the notification. What she saw made her vomit right in the parking lot. Cooper finally got to the tiny house, and a medium build brunette was with him.

Chapter 15

Just that morning, the proximity of the two houses she was watching and how little time it took to get between them made her nervous. Now, she was thankful it would take minutes to get from one to the other.

During the brief drive, images of what that man was doing with that woman made her cringe on the outside as much as on the inside. Yes, Cooper was a "smooth" man, and things might start consensual, but it didn't make her cringe any less. Sure enough, the second rental car was parked in the driveway with, she assumed, the woman's little Prius alongside. Looping around to the other side of the street, she made sure to park close enough for the walkie-talkies to work but far enough not to be seen.

You know, it's not talked about much, but from an unbiased point of view, it's quite easy to tell when a woman is faking things for the sake of a man's ego, and this poor woman was no actress. Chelsea sat there uncomfortably, not wanting to record any unnecessary theatrics, but also not wanting to risk this woman's life, waiting to hear if things turned malevolent.

Sitting there, listening to everything and everywhere they went (was she the only person who thought kitchen "encounters" were just plain icky?), Chelsea began to think this was all a huge mistake. In the report, those women looked like much more happened to them than what was happening inside. She was about to lean back and purposefully zone out on the ceiling when movement down the street caught her attention.

A normal person riding their bike down a residential street was not uncommon, and Chelsea wouldn't have thought anything of it if that was all they were doing. But once they were three houses away, they got off the bike, leaned it against the mailbox, and the person began walking back up the street. That was not what a normal person would do, especially at night.

Turning off the awkward sound effects from the walkie-talkie, Chelsea slid as far down in her seat as she could while keeping her eyes on this stranger. Then, she saw it. As he got to the Prius, he slid down to tie his shoe, placing his hand on the car for support getting up, planting a tracking device on her car.

Watching him carefully, she noticed two things before he walked past her car and down a few more houses before doubling back and riding away. First, his shoes were so white they practically glowed in the dark. That didn't match any of the Back Road Boys' fashion sense. They were more the semi-formal or comfort shoe type of guys. Second, this man had a slight lean to the left when he walked, indicating a sore back or maybe even a shorter leg.

There was no more time to think about her mystery man, for Chelsea's phone buzzed, indicating someone was exiting the tiny house. Sure enough, Miss Prius was done putting on a show and at the front door, not too happy with the night's ending. Flipping the walkie-talkie back on, Chelsea heard a few choice words before seeing the poor woman, who put so much effort into the night, huff down the driveway and towards her little car. Quickly scanning the area, Mystery Man was nowhere to be found.

Without even thinking, Chelsea quickly turned on the car, put it in gear, and raced over to block the woman from leaving. She wasn't sure if this would work, but it was worth a shot. Chelsea got out of her car and grabbed both of their attention.

"So, I guess I'm replaceable, just like that, if I happen to be a little late?" With her heavy accent and a hand on her hip, she watched the smug look on Cooper's face fall away. Even in the dim porch light, Chelsea could tell he paled.

"Tina! What the hell are you doing here?" Miss Prius did a slow turn back towards Cooper. "Who the hell is she?" Again, the poor woman."Oh, I was his original date for the night, but he can find exactly what he wants anywhere he goes. Or am I no longer 'exactly what you hoped to find'?""Oh, hell no! You jackass!" Miss Prius turned on Cooper, but he didn't know when to keep his smart mouth shut. "You didn't have a problem with my ass earlier."A shriek and flailing arms pursued Cooper, giving Chelsea the distraction needed. It took her some time to locate the tracking device; she would have missed it if she didn't see exactly where it had been placed. With the bug in her hand, all felt right in the world again until she heard, "What are you doing to my car!?"

Standing up and jingling her keys, Chelsea already had a response. "Oh, don't mind me. I dropped my keys, is all."

"Well, you have your keys now, so move your sorry-ass car out of my way so I can get out of here." The biting words were directed towards Chelsea, but she knew the jaded response was due to Cooper, not her…hopefully. What Chelsea did was give a quick smile and turn towards her car. Chelsea thought, "Geez, Cooper sure knows how to pick them," until she remembered she was his first choice for a date tonight.

Chelsea only took a few seconds to get in and move her car, just enough for the Prius to book it out of the driveway. The woman's driving was as angry as her words. It was a good thing most of the neighbors parked in their driveway, or the woman would have likely sideswiped one, and having the cops present was the last thing Chelsea needed.

Shaking slightly, Chelsea sat in her idling car with Cooper in the driveway. Her mind spun with everything that took place over the past few minutes.

Some Mystery Man just marked Cooper's date. But just because someone else kept Miss Prius' car didn't mean Cooper wasn't the serial killer. It could tell he had some outside help. The file didn't say anything about a suspected second person, but that didn't make it impossible or even unlikely. She should call the Chief, but this was only speculation until proof could be found.

This made her head spin. Wanting to guess no longer or second guess what was going on, Chelsea looked at Cooper and hoped his answer to her question would be honest.

Chelsea rolled down her window and asked, "So, that's what you do? Bring strange women over to your 'love shack' and kick them out as soon as you're done?" Her voice was as tired and confused as she felt. His response, though, was just as cocky as ever."No, sometimes I call the good ones and ask if they want to come over again."Chelsea's jaw dropped as she stared at him, at a loss for words. She *had* hoped for honesty.Cooper didn't even have the decency to feign remorse. "Maybe if I had a woman like you, I wouldn't be like this."

Oh, dear gussy, this man knew no shame. Rolling her eyes in genuine disgust, Chelsea put the car in drive and left while clutching the hard, cold tracking device. Miss Prius was safe, for now. Chelsea could only hope she stayed that way.

Chapter 16

The best way to disable a tracking device is the same way to guarantee any electronics' demise: water. Rummaging through the debris on the passenger side floor, an old coffee cup and a half-drunk plastic water bottle were eventually found. Careful not to spill on herself, she watched and waited for the little red light to stop glowing. It was an unusual tracker, but Chelsea would have to take a closer look a little later. Once the tracker was dead, Chelsea needed to locate Miss Prius to ensure she was still alive.

It was Chelsea's only locator left and was meant to go on Cooper's vehicle, but it found its new home under a silver Prius. Following the woman north and further from the mountain, Chelsea eventually stopped in front of two completely average houses in an unimpressive neighborhood. Everything was cookie-cutter and earth-tone.

But that didn't bother Chelsea. Not compared with Miss Prius having a neighbor with an identical car. It wasn't unheard of, but boy, was it inconvenient. Trying to think of any tell-tale signs that belonged to her, Chelsea closed her eyes and tried remembering the scene.

Chelsea didn't remember anything on the vehicle's exterior that could help identify it, but she did remember seeing something hanging from the rear-view mirror. Rummaging through her bag in the back, Chelsea quickly grabbed a hoodie and threw it on. Taking a gamble, she walked right past both driveways.

The right driveway had a motion-activated light. Circling the small block, Chelsea made it back and stopped in the left neighbor's driveway. She looked through the windshield.

Nothing. Her tracker must be on the other car. But she couldn't get to the car or get close enough to read the license plate. If she tried, it would be too obvious, and who knows if there were snoopy neighbors about. No, she needed to get her tracker back, but not here. She needed someplace more populated. She needed to distinguish that Prius from any other Prius. She needed to see what was in the rearview mirror.

Picking up a rock in the zero-scape yard, Chelsea threw it again to activate the driveway light. Staying in the shadows, Chelsea slinked to the nearside of the driveway. Looking across the narrow sideyard to the other Prius, Chelsea saw an intricate, if not flashy, purple dream catcher with long brown and white feathers perfectly lit by the light.

That would certainly catch Chelsea's attention the next time she saw it.

Once back in her car, Chelsea sat there, unsure what her next step should be. Should she knock on the door and explain to the woman what was happening? That, whoever she was, was in the middle of a murder investigation and Chelsea had some questions for her? Or should Chelsea at least warn her, again, about going home with strange men? Or should Chelsea not say anything? Did Chelsea need to sneak around and put eyes and ears on this woman, or had the moment of danger passed?

Twenty minutes elapsed while Chelsea visually ran through every scenario in her mind, only to have them all end disastrously. It seemed the best move right now was to do nothing.

Unsatisfied with her decision but happy that no one else knew where Miss Prius lived, Chelsea pulled up her current location and wrote down Miss Prius' address, just in case. With that, Chelsea was once again on the road. This time, to find a place where she could sit and mull over the questions surrounding Mystery Man.

Chapter 17

Chelsea felt safe enough to pull over and examine the tracker in only one place: the outskirts of a crowded Walmart parking lot. Putting distance between her and the large mass of cars and customers gave her privacy, but being around so many witnesses (not to mention parking lot cameras) meant her risk of being attacked was at a minimum.

Chelsea gave the tracker a good look-over. It was one she had seen online and even bought before. That was back before her cases became more complicated, and pinpoint accuracy on her targets was important.

This device couldn't show you more than which house or office building it was near or if a target was on the move. But although this was more of a toy than serious spyware, this guy was no amateur. She had seen him place it in a way and place that suggested he had done it many times before. On top of that, you could get these trackers for only a few bucks. God only knew how many the man had out there.

That thought made Chelsea's blood run cold. Not just because of the thought of an outsider following the Back Road Boys around the country and murdering women associated with them but because the Back Road Boys had been to more than the thirteen locations linked to murder cases. Many, many more.

Her phone notification went off, startling Chelsea out of her thoughts. The picture that popped up showed Cooper leaving the house. "That took long enough."

Flipping through the photos, she saw no one else had gone to or from the property since Chelsea's little interruption. Checking her other tracking devices, Chelsea noticed the Back

Road Boys' other vehicle was still at the big house, and Miss Prius was still at home.

Chelsea patted herself on the back for not only taking the stalker's tracking device but thinking of replacing it with her own, but that left her with the problem of the Back Road Boy's second car. She *needed* that second tracker.

Another problem presented itself tonight as well. The suspect list now grew to six people, one with no name, no face, and only a pair of bright shoes and a slight hitch in his step to identify him. That didn't give her much to go on, especially if this was some random person following the group around the country. After all, many people are sore from flights, drives, and hotel beds.

A hotel bed. That sounded pretty good to her right now. The adrenalin rush from her crazy night was wearing off and fast.

A quick internet search later, Chelsea found a cheap motel. Within twenty minutes, she was in a room resembling a horror movie scene and smelled like an ashtray. It was safe to say she would never recommend that place to anyone, especially those with breathing issues or traveling with small children.

Turning on the TV for comfort measures, Chelsea wished more than anything to be with her little girl. She spent the rest of the night reminding herself this was all worth it if it meant not having to leave home again.

Chapter 18

As soon as Chelsea was rested enough to drive safely, she semi-fled that motel and sat down to an early breakfast of coffee and hotcakes at a big-name pancake place. She always thought it best caffeinated, and if she had a full stomach, she wouldn't be so tempted to snack and leave her rental a mess.

Doing things old school, Chelsea pulled Cooper's file along with her large notebook and began making some edits to the notes on the Back Road Boys. They were as follows:

<u>FIND WHITE SHOESWATCH FOR LIMPGET SECOND TRACKER FROM PRIUS</u>

<u>Kevin and Austin</u> aren't committed to their marriages, and extra female attention is high on their radar. However, they also seemed very emasculated. That could fuel rage in a man, but it could also break them enough that they wouldn't be able to stand up to a woman, let alone do what the perpetrator did.

<u>Jonathan</u> – supposedly has a fiancé but won't show her off. Organized and tech-savvy enough to plan something like this, with such rigorous schedules, job demands, and personal restraints, this could be a chaotic mental release. People skills unknown. Most physically fit of the five men. Restraining a woman and being able to relocate her body to a remote place would be easy enough.

<u>Zech</u> – It was a struggle for her to imagine his motives, but she could think of a few. Although they looked truly happy, Zech and Miriam had rough patches, and his business trips were one of them. He was a good father, but he was never engaged, even when he was home. Lexi being there so often probably didn't help much. And he always *Always* looked forward to leaving. With a guilty conscience, Chelsea went back to her notes.

<u>Zech</u> - Could easily pick up a woman if he wanted to. His loyalty could be too good to be true. Willingly participates in stealing company money by renting a house. He knows everyone else's secrets and could use them to his advantage: leverage, personal gain, freedom.

<u>Cooper</u> – Still #1 suspect. See file.

Chelsea sat back in her booth seat and exhaled a long, exacerbated breath. She was dissatisfied, and for all she knew, any one of them, or all of them, were involved in the murders.

Ping! Chelsea was not quite ready for the day to begin, but begin it must. She picked up her phone and looked at the notifications.

The Back Road Boys were on the move—time to make a dent in the suspect list. Chelsea's fourth cup of coffee was a good indicator of how crappy a night she had, so she reasoned a second breaking-and-entering was physically and mentally out of the question. Her exhaustion made it too risky to put more eyes and ears on the big house, and that only left tailing and gathering intel.

Too bad there was nothing on the itinerary saying who would take which job today. All Chelsea knew was that Cooper wouldn't be there unless it were somewhere important.

Chelsea sat back, shoved a few more bites of her hotcakes in her mouth, and paid her bill while watching the little red dot on her phone move throughout the city.

It finally stopped. Looking up the location, Chelsea saw it was a small, run-down, private car lot. That was a relief. Chelsea wanted to rule out the other guys before focusing on Cooper, and if this car stopped at a small lot, that meant someone other than Cooper was in that vehicle.

Ping! Miss Prius was on the move, too, and headed in the other direction. Chelsea needed that tracker, but the small car lot was closer.

Snaking her way through town, Chelsea finally stopped near a car lot that had seen better years. The location was great, and the cars available were in nice condition, but the uneven cement, dust-covered lot, and dingy shed they called an office made buyers drive on to the next place. That was too bad. With a small investment in his property, the man could have a booming business.

Chelsea stayed across the road until she could see who took this work call. To her surprise, Jonathan and not Kevin or Austin were speaking with the owner. Referencing her notebook, she was distressed over how little she had on the man, which meant she had no idea how to approach him. However, she still had an advantage; he had never seen her before. Well, to her knowledge, anyway. And if he had never seen her, she needed to make a big first impression.

Riffling through her luggage in the back, she covertly changed her top to something more eye-catching.

Jonathan and the owner must have been completely engrossed in their conversation, for neither noticed Chelsea was on the lot and looking at vehicles. That was good because until Chelsea nearly walked into them, she got to see a side of Jonathan she didn't think he had. Chelsea also noticed he walked with a slight limp.

"I told you, I don't want to sell." The older man was trying to look like he was working while walking away from Jonathan, but Jonathan stayed at his heels and wouldn't take no for an answer. "And yet that doesn't change your position or the numbers. You have two weeks left before debts are due and no way to meet them, even if you sold every car on the lot."The owner turned on Jonathan, red-faced and fuming. "You can't strong-arm me. Those are private documents, and you stole them! I'll call the authorities on you!" "And if you do, I'll also show them these." Jonathan's deadly cold voice spoke volumes, and the owner's face instantly changed from red to white.

Chelsea couldn't see what Jonathan was showing him, but if it could deflate the angered owner that quickly, there was no way he would call the cops on Jonathan.

Jonathan's tech skills were good, and he was nothing like the nerd she pictured. This man commanded the conversation, and "no" was not an answer he allowed. Aggression, strength, limp, her nausea. It was all lining up.

Jonathan lowered his threatening paper and spoke in a more pleasant voice, "Now, about the newer models, specifically anything less than five years old, I-"That's when the owner finally noticed Chelsea. "Oh, miss. Miss!" he called out and nearly ran over to her.

Chelsea must have wandered a little too close while doing her mental checklist, for before she knew it, both men were at her side, one to sell a car and one to get her off the lot. Turning to the owner, she kindly asked to see an accident report regarding a decent, sporty car in the far back corner. Happy to have a customer, the owner quickly left to do her bidding to get away from Jonathan. Chelsea wasted no time turning her attention to Jonathan.

"I must say, car salesmen are getting easier on the eyes. Almost as good as the cars they sell. Have you worked here long?" Chelsea's voice was low and honey-sweet. She even threw in a little lip chewing to make an impression. Clearing his throat, obviously uncomfortable with the attention given him, Jonathan gave Chelsea a quick and awkward look over before answering.

"I don't work here. Mr. Kerns is the only employee right now." Even without the fidgeting and lack of eye contact, Chelsea could see Jonathan was instantly uncomfortable being left alone with her.

This was a revelation. Putting her theory to the test, Chelsea made a show of sighing and pouted. "Oh, that's too bad. I'd be much more willing to take you for a test drive."

She knew she was laying it on thick, but he seemed to crumble under her advances. "Um, well, I…"

"I have those papers for you, miss!" Mr. Kerns had the worst timing.

The interruption was rewarded with an audible sigh of relief from Jonathan. Despite the force he showed Mr. Kerns not two minutes ago, he was nothing but a bundle of insecurity now.

Chelsea smiled at the owner. "Thank you so much," she said in a more genuine voice than she felt, "but I just got a call and can't stay." Turning to Jonathan, she handed him her burner's phone number on a napkin and added, "Let me know if you ever have time for that test drive." With a wink, Chelsea left a visibly shaken Jonathan and an enraged Mr. Kerns to finish their discussion.

Chapter 19

In the safety of her car, not long after, Chelsea pulled over at a nearby fast-food joint and took out her notebook again. In Jonathan's section, Chelsea added: Tech wiz, likely connected to the darknet. Only aggressive towards men/uncomfortable around forward women. Has a limp.

It was obvious Jonathan didn't have much confidence around women. This didn't mean he wasn't guilty of tracking a woman's car. Jonathan Thomas could do some very sketchy tech stuff from what she had just witnessed. Yet how he handled himself around her just now…she could swear in front of a jury without hesitation that he didn't have the confidence to move on a woman who was throwing herself at him, let alone be the initiator. And the confidence necessary to do those horrific acts done to all those women…no, he couldn't be the murderer. That was good for him and Chelsea; Jonathan was crossed off her mental suspect list. But the limp? Well, maybe he was innocent of murder, but perhaps he wasn't quite in the clear.

Chelsea's phone buzzed, interrupting her Jonathan conundrum. The front door camera verified Cooper was yet again at the tiny home and wasn't alone. This man sure knew how to get around a town. Just thinking about that made her want to contact every known woman he's been with and warn them to get tested.

Chelsea would have gladly broken up their afternoon delight to save that woman's future heartache, whether it was from an unfortunate test result or from, well, death-by-serial-killer. Still, she noticed the car in the driveway. The one she needed eyes on.

Chelsea knew the walkie-talkie batteries were long dead, so there was no reason to get within hearing range. That left only one thing for her to do, and unfortunately, it was out of the way. Well, Chelsea needed to get the tracker anyway.

Chelsea wrote down a quick description of the woman she saw entering the house and prayed she would never see the woman again, especially not in one of her files.

Chapter 20

The Prius tracker led Chelsea to a shopping district that catered to the more financially strained class. Whether she worked in the area or was only there to shop, there was no way to tell, but it didn't make much of a difference to Chelsea. All she wanted was to get in and get out without being seen. There was always the "Oh my God, you shop here too?!" response if they accidentally bumped into each other, but she hoped it wouldn't come to that.

Considering the number of cars in the parking lot, there was little foot traffic. That was good and bad. The good thing was few witnesses. The bad thing was the Baader-Meinhof Phenomenon. Chelsea was looking for a Prius, and so she saw Priuses everywhere. To make things worse, she forgot to write down the license plate last night. Thank goodness Chelsea had another way to identify the car.

Weaving through the parking lot, trying to look like she was on her way somewhere and not just snooping on vehicles, Chelsea's eyes darted back and forth, hungrily searching for the dream catcher.

The parking lot was quite large, and it took Chelsea seven minutes to locate the purple and brown dream catcher in the sea of cars, but there was an issue. It was in one of the parking spots directly in front of a nail salon, music store, and clothing outlet.

This was a less-than-ideal location. The stores had large, reflective windows looking out, constant in-and-out customer traffic and several people walking up and down. With this many people around and no way to tell if someone was looking at her from inside one of the stores, Chelsea decided it was time to do the shoe trick again.

Chelsea kept walking past the car until she found a public restroom. Once inside, she undid one of her shoelaces, carefully strode back to the Prius, knelt, and did her thing. However, she heard a most unexpected greeting before her laces were taut.

"Drop your keys again?" Not wanting to look up but unable to do anything else, Chelsea covered her eyes from the glaring sun and saw Miss Prius standing above her, arms crossed, her eyes and voice lethal.

Chelsea didn't like her position or the other woman's body language. It also looked to Chelsea that Miss Prius' explosive behavior last night may not have been out of her norm.

Miss Prius looked away and huffed. Licking her teeth behind her lips, she cocked her head to the side and half-growled, half-whispered, "I would kick you in the face right now, but my boss is watching, and I need to keep this job.""Well, that's a relief," Chelsea said honestly, "I want you to keep your job too."Not laughing at Chelsea's wit, the woman gestured to Chelsea's hand and demanded, "What did you just take off my car?"

Chelsea didn't believe the woman was ready for the answer. Then again, she also thought her shoe-tying trick was executed perfectly. "I can tell you and explain everything," Chelsea offered, "but it might take a longer break than your boss is okay with."

Behind Miss Prius, someone from the nearby nail salon called, "Val? Is everything okay?""Yeah, Deb," Miss Prius, who Chelsea deduced was Val, yelled back. After a second's thought, Val added, "I'm going on my lunch."

Narrowing her eyes at Chelsea, Val said in a cold voice, "Well, looky there, we have time now. So come with me, or I'll kick your teeth in."

Thinking Val would make good on her threat, Chelsea stood and followed Val a few stores down to a small soup and sandwich shop. Without waiting for a hostess, Val led them to a corner booth and pointed for Chelsea to sit down in the corner with Val between her and the exit.

Sitting down across from her, Val plopped down and crossed her arms. "Okay, Butterfingers, spill."

It was so different being on this side of an interrogation. First with Chief Jordan, now with Val. When were the tables going to stop turning?

There was just no way to get around what was about to happen. Chelsea took a big breath and began.

"My name is Chelsea Markwell. The city of Tulsa commissioned me, OK, to spy on Cooper Gray regarding the kidnapping, torture, and murder of at least thirteen women. I took a tracker off your vehicle last night and replaced it with my own," Chelsea showed the tracker between her forefinger and thumb, "to make sure you were safe, and now I've come to take it back because I need to put it on Cooper's second car that is at his second house."

Val began to glare at her from the beginning. What Chelsea first thought would be a shocker for the woman ended up making her, what? Mad? Offended? Either way, she was not taking this news how Chelsea expected.

"Do you think I'm an idiot or something?"Chelsea was taken a little by surprise with the question. "Well, I wouldn't say you're an idiot, but I didn't think you would-""I heard him call you Tina last night." Val's interruption was forceful and a bit upsetting to Chelsea, but she could see how Val would be confused."Well… yes." Chelsea slowly explained, "I'm spying on him. Cooper. As in, undercover? Of course, I wouldn't tell him my real-""And you said you had a date with him earlier that night. A spy going on a date with the person they're spying on? I don't think so." Val's smug look and interruption weren't nearly as forgivable this time. Val didn't understand and didn't want to. Even if Chelsea could get a full sentence around this woman, it was beginning to look like it wouldn't matter anyway.

Chelsea said quickly, "I need people to talk, and that means interacting with them. Professionally. You can't expect-" "You're just jealous of me."

Okay, this was getting out of hand.

"Val," Chelsea tried to explain. "Valerie.""Okay, Valerie." Chelsea's sarcasm meant her composure was beginning to slip a little, but who knows what damage would be done if she didn't get this woman on her side. Or what she would tell Cooper.

But the woman was irritating, and Chelsea was wasting time. "Valerie, I just came here to take my tracker back. So, if you'll excuse me, I need to get back to my job; following Cooper and his men."

Chelsea made the mistake of repeatedly showing the tracking device while talking. Valerie practically flew off her seat, lunging for the device, but she was one second too late. Instead of swiping the device, one of Valerie's excessively long nails clipped the back of Chelsea's hand.

It was bad enough that Valerie wouldn't listen, but getting accused of jealousy *and* getting maimed was more than Chelsea could take.

"I told you, I wanted to make sure you were safe. I even took a different tracking device off your car, so you're welcome." Rubbing the back of her hand and examining the part where a little piece of skin was no longer there, Chelsea added, "Did you have to do that just now?"

Valerie didn't care, or maybe she didn't hear. But instead of responding the way Chelsea thought, Valerie pointed her bright acrylic nail at Chelsea and squawked, "Are you tracking Cooper too?!""No! Did you not…ugh!" With Chelsea's composure now completely gone, it took all her patience not to jump the table and shake some sense into this woman.

"Did you not hear anything I just said? I told you I needed to take this one Off YOUR car and put it On COOPERS. Because He Might. Be. A. Murderer!!!"Valerie didn't even flinch at those words. Instead, she chirped, "I'm calling him right now.""What!"

Whipping out her phone, Valerie began to text in a flurry. Chelsea could do only one thing, and it was another first. Swiping the phone, Chelsea flew out of her seat and was near the door before Valerie knew what was happening.

Silently praying Valerie wore poor running shoes, Chelsea bolted to her rental car and was safely inside it before Valerie caught up and pounded on the window.

"You crazy bitch! You thief! Give that back!!" Valerie shrieked those sentences all the while. Chelsea repeatedly yelled back, "I'm sorry, I'm sorry!"

Before giving Valerie a chance to jump on top of the car or get the attention of the cops, Chelsea turned the engine over and drove away as safely as possible, Valerie trailing her to the end of the parking row.

Chapter 21

Once Chelsea hit the open road, she began breathing again. Glancing down at the bejeweled phone on her lap, Chelsea couldn't believe what she just did. And it wasn't even 1 pm!

Stress manifests itself differently depending on the person. With Chelsea, stress caused her to talk to herself out loud.

It started as a mumble and continued to get louder, "And just like that, I added theft, in broad daylight, to my firsts. Oh, and don't forget about telling some psycho woman my full, real name, along with leaving a freaking DNA sample! Yeah, I'm just *loving* these firsts!!!"

Once Chelsea began talking to herself, it was hard for her to stop. "I can just see Chief now. 'Why did you get arrested in Phoenix again?' 'Oh, you know, just robbing a lady who was about to tip off the killer about me spying on him.' You're killing this, Cece!" By the time she ended, Chelsea was practically yelling at herself.

The last thing Chelsea wanted to hear was her phone's announcement of Cooper and his newest lady leaving the house. Crap, she wouldn't make it in time. Chelsea did a quick drive-by at the big house without bothering to stop by the tiny house, hoping Cooper would drive straight there.

No such luck. Cooper was once again lost in the wind. As for the woman he was just with, there was no way of knowing what happened to her. Or if she, too, fell victim to one of Mystery Man's tracking devices.

Parked across the street from the house, feeling every bit the failure, Chelsea's groan turned into a yell of rage. Her entire day felt wasted; everything in that shopping mall could have ruined her, and she wasn't even that happy to have her tracking device back because she still couldn't put the blasted thing to use. The only positive thing Chelsea could think of was that now Valerie could not communicate with Cooper.

Well, Chelsea tried to see that as a positive, but the *way* it happened? The way she went about it? It made Chelsea question who she was turning into. For instance, until now, she would have never stolen another woman's phone, let alone purposefully break into it.

That's what Chelsea was thinking when she opened up Valerie's messages. Fortunately for Chelsea, Valerie used a swipe password, and her finger marks were still visible on the dark screen. Cracking her code was as easy as could be.

From the looks of it, Chelsea took the phone just in time. There, in the messaging app, was the sentence, *"Crazy lady here. Says you killed people-"*. It was promptly erased.

Scrolling to the beginning of the thread, it looked like Cooper met Valerie Morana at lunch shortly after telling Tina Bennet where his tiny house was located. There were quite a few racy messages and photos exchanged between the two. Chelsea tried to scan over those as best she could. However, a few images would be burned into Chelsea's memory forever.

Near the end of their conversation, one thread caught her attention. Valerie told Cooper she was working tonight and asked if he wanted to drop by when she got off. . He did, of course. But there was nothing else in the message to indicate where.,That was strange. Chelsea looked , but there were no phone calls to Cooper, and no other apps used to communicate with him.. It's possible Valerie could have erased some of her messages, but why tell someone to meet you without giving a place or time?

Chelsea doubted Valerie was talking about her job at the shopping center. No, she must have told Cooper about where she has a second job sometime in person last night.

Chelsea began to pound on the steering wheel. Where Valerie and Cooper were supposed to meet was impossible for Chelsea to find, thanks to her taking the tracker off the Prius.

After allowing herself the time to vent her frustration and feelings of doubt, Chelsea wiped some angry tears off her face and pulled out her cell phone.

This was beyond her skills. Chelsea was in more over her head now than at the Dallas call center, Vancouver dairy farm, and Reno casino jobs all rolled into one. And those were quite unbelievable experiences.

Desperate, Chelsea needed help. More than that, she needed Joe. The phone only rang twice before Joe picked up.

"Hey Chelsea, I thought you were on some big, bad job for the Chief.""I am." Chelsea's short response spoke volumes.

"… What's wrong?" Chelsea could hear the strain on the other line and kicked herself for the position she was about to put him in.

Shaking her head, Chelsea closed her eyes and pinched the bridge of her nose while continuing, "A lot, but I can't tell you anything. At least not until I know if you can help me."

"Okay," Joe asked, "So, if I *can* help, you can tell me what's wrong, but if I can't, then what?"

"Then I promise to fill you in when I get home."

Chelsea heard Joe huff on the other end, but she knew Joe wouldn't take her professional boundaries personally.

"Okay, Chelsea, what do you need?" Joe asked it rather flatly, but it made the corners of Chelsea's lips turn up ever so slightly. She knew she could count on him.

"If I gave you an address, could you give me a name and background information, like where they work and stuff?"The brief pause on the other end was answer enough. Joe's response only proved her suspicion.

"I assume you're not in Tulsa, so no. And even if you *were* in Tulsa, not really."

The sign on her end was long and heavy. "Okay."

That was all she could say.

"Chelsea? Is everything okay?"*No,* she thought. Longing to tell him everything, her fears, the stress, the job she knew she couldn't finish in only two more days…

Two more days. That's all the time she had left. She had no new evidence to add to the file except what might be happening at a meeting that may or may not happen in a location she has no way of finding. Her brain practically screamed at her, *"NO, everything was not okay, and I will never be forced into a case like this again!"*

But that was not how she could answer her Joe. To reassure her friend, Chelsea cleared her throat and asked in a cheerful way that sounded fake even to Joe's ears, "For now, things could be better, but they could also be worse. I was just wondering if you could help speed things up for me. I only have two more days left to get some information, and I'm no further along now than when I first arrived."

"And where is 'here' this time?" There was a slight accusation in that question.

Chelsea always told Joe where she was going. It was a safety net put in place unless something went wrong. One thing she trusted Joe with over her sister.

But Chief specifically told her not to tell Joe, and she was forced to comply."I'm so sorry, Joe. Chief said he couldn't risk any particulars of this case to get leaked. If they did, he swore up and down he wouldn't pay me, and there would be repercussions for those I spoke with. And to be honest, this is a really big case. I understand why he can't afford to let any of this leak out."

"What? Chels, he can't not pay you! And do you think I would let something this secretive slip out after all the other secrets I've kept over the years?"

Joe didn't realize it then, so he didn't think about how those words hurt Chelsea. True, she had kept many secrets in her life, and Joe was privileged to hear most. Including the one she regretted most.

But Joe wasn't speaking of *that* secret. Chelsea just mistook it that way. Joe continued rattling on over the phone.

 "What about your safety? What would happen to Lexi if you didn't come home? What do I do if you up and disappear!? ""It's not me disappearing that I'm worried about!" Chelsea didn't mean to yell at Joe; it just came out. "Secrets! Secrets, Joe, are what I'm afraid of!"

Silence lingered over the line. Chelsea was desperate for anyone to help her share the burden of the case, but Joe couldn't be allowed to know the details. Not this time. And the secrecy was killing them both.

Joe sighed on the other end of the line. Chelsea could practically see him pinching the bridge of his nose and shaking his head at her. "At least tell me, Chelsea, are *you* okay? Are you safe?"

Chelsea's sigh was enough of a "no" for Joe not to need an answer. He wondered what other information he could glean just by talking with her instead of bluntly asking. But that would be intrusive, and with everything he was going through with Haley…. No, he didn't need to add anything more to his plate that wasn't his responsibility.

"I didn't snoop, Chelsea, but people are talking. Not about you, but about something big going on in Tulsa. Is it true? Are people disappearing?""…I can't tell you, Joe." Chelsea's voice was strangled. Silence was again the only thing Chelsea heard on the other end of the line. "I need this case, Joe. And after I'm back and tell you everything, you'll understand why I just can't now."

"Are you really that strapped for money?" Joe's voice had a tinge of sadness and urgency in it. Something Chelsea rarely heard from him, and she didn't like it. "Let me help, Chels. Now that Haley-""No, it's more than about the money. And since you already said you couldn't help, I need to find someone who can." That stung even her ears. Chelsea realized a little too late she had cut him off, and he was just about to say something regarding Haley, too. Chelsea had forgotten to inquire about his sick wife before leaving town. Seeing how selfish of a friend she had been over the last few months if not years, made Chelsea question herself and her choices.

"I'm sorry, Joe, I-.""No, I get it." It was Joe's turn to cut her off, but he couldn't say everything he wanted; everythingweighing him down.

Chelsea bit her tongue, held her breath, and waited for Joe to break the dense silence. She wanted him to say something;

anything! Surely whatever he had to say would be better than this void between them. "I'll see you in three days, Chelsea."

He used her full name. He hung up. He was gone.She now felt more alone than ever.

Chapter 22

Valerie's phone was on silent, so Chelsea was unaware of all the calls and messages coming in during her chat with Joe and the time she took to recuperate. When Chelsea looked at the device again, she was parked near the big house, waiting for the Back Road Boys to come home.

Of course, Valerie would be trying to locate her phone. Quickly disabling its location, Chelsea perused the tasteless message thread again and even laughed at some descriptive imagery. Chelsea had to remind herself this wasn't funny and this woman's safety was still her priority.

"Messages," Chelsea whispered to herself. Why worry over something happening later when she could stop it right now?

After getting a taste for the woman's vocabulary and messaging style, Chelsea sent a quick text to Cooper insisting they get together before she started work tonight instead of after. He replied within a minute, saying he'd be happy to make that happen. She ignored the details given on what to expect during their rendezvous.

There was a catch, though. Cooper was no longer interested in meeting at the tiny house. He wanted to go to her place. *"I showed you mine. You show me yours."* Thank goodness he was talking about homes. She told him no and offered the horror motel site instead.

Turning Cooper down resulted in a cease of messages. He must not be used to a woman telling him no. That was fine with Chelsea for now. She was ready for food, and Chelsea didn't properly think things through. After all, what would she have done if Cooper had said yes? Chelsea had no idea when Cooper would show up without a tracker on the car. There was no need to call the cops since he wasn't paying for services (that she knew of). If Cooper had said yes, it would have probably made a bigger mess of things.

As if the heavens opened, and at least one of her prayers was heard and answered, both company cars pulled up to the big house with some bags of local fast food. With both cars parked side by side, Chelsea was prepared to hop out as soon as they were inside and place the tracker on the second car. But something looked off to Chelsea.

Chelsea quickly inserted her earbuds as soon as they were through the door. Her hunger subsided as she anxiously listened in.

"We're back! If your food order's wrong, suck it. That place was a mess, and I ain't going back because one of you wants extra pickles, no mustard, a different side, or just can't stomach what you ordered." Kevin's voice sounded tired. She had no idea what all their work deals entailed, but she didn't think it would be difficult enough to render such an attitude. "I missed you too." Was Zech's reply. But he shouldn't have missed them at all…

If Chelsea could have printed a transcript of the following conversation, it would have gone like this:

Jonathan: "Man, Zech, you're always sick when we're on a trip."Zech: "No, I'm not, only now and then."Kevin: "No, man, it's been a lot lately. What, your soft stomach can't handle all this *delicious* fast food?"Zech: "Something like that. Not everyone can have a stomach of iron like you, Kevin."Kevin: "Well, at least I don't waste most of the day cramping like a menstruating girl."Chorus of laughter. Zech: "Hey, I still got plenty of work done from here. At least more than you, Cooper."Cooper: "Yeah, I'm sure you did."

Chelsea couldn't see what gesture was being met with the chorus of laughter, but she could guess. However, what startled her more than their behavior was knowing Zech had been sitting inside the house while she threw herself a pity party earlier.

Did Zech see her? If she could guess, Zech's voice's calm and natural sound told her he hadn't. But that was being careless, and she needed to be more careful.

Austin: "Jonathan, what happened to your leg?"*Yes, Jonathan, what did happen to your leg?*Jonathan: "That privately owned lot you sent me to today? Yeah, the lot is covered in potholes. I twisted my ankle as soon as I stepped foot on the place. He's lucky he signed the papers after a fleeting customer came by. If he didn't, I would have threatened a lawsuit and *still* sued him after he signed the cars over to us just for pissing me off."*How aggressive. That would explain the limp, though. Darn.*Jonathan: "And you two, how did we do with the PD fleet?Kevin: "They didn't want to agree to our terms, but Austin was there to smooth things out. Man, I hate cops. You should have known better than sending me over there."Cooper: "That's why I didn't send you alone. I needed Jonathan at the private lot, Zech crapped out on us again, and I had a private engagement."*Yes you did, perv.*Austin: "And since I did such a good job, I'm going to enjoy the spoils of war. The place is mine tonight, guys."The statement was met with much opposition.Cooper: "Okay, okay, okay! Now everybody, calm down. We all but met our quota. Austin, did you already make plans tonight?"Austin: "Making them right now."Cooper: "Fine. Jonathan and Kevin, we have one place to go tomorrow, and it doesn't require all of us. Since Zech looks like shit, I guess Austin and I can take it. So, figure out who gets the morning and afternoon and do what you want with the place. But it's mine Friday morning. Understood?"

Chelsea pulled her earbuds out then. Like the alpha dog he was, Cooper had no problem telling his underlings even what times they were allowed to woo and prey on women. Chelsea was so disgusted by them all that if she had anything in her stomach, she would purposefully purge herself.

When Chelsea arrived, five days felt like a long time to wrap up this case. But it was now Wednesday night. She had tomorrow and Friday morning to get something concrete. This called for a gutsy move. One she was hesitant and downright dreading to make. Whipping out Valerie's phone, she went for it.

"Okay, my place. I can't tonight or tomorrow. Friday morning?"Chelsea waited, unsure of which answer she wanted. *"Can't wait. Just tell me where."*

Chelsea didn't dare send Valerie's real address but instead sent Cooper one from a local real estate listing. If his showing up at an empty house didn't bruise his pride, nothing would.

"Friday it is," was his only response. Neither of them bothered texting after that.

Putting her earbuds back in, Chelsea kept an ear out while doing her shoe-tying car tag. She knew Cooper got and answered her message, but he didn't say anything to the guys. That was odd, him being the type of man who would usually rub it in their faces. But they were also busy talking about other things, and maybe he didn't want to be teased for having a recycled woman.

Chapter 23

Chelsea sat in her car. The choking summer-like heat belied the early autumn season typical in most other states. A whole other day had gone by with no success in any such meaning of the word. Boring tailings, stale coffee, nearly inedible drive-thru food, and sleepless nights peppered her last 30 hours, and now she sat, waiting. Waitingfor her date and waiting to meet her supposed serial killer. Waiting to get out of the spy business once and for all. Why was she waiting so long?The sky darkened too quickly. The parking lot at the head of the mountain trail that was lit and full of cars was now empty, deserted, void of life and light. Nearly dripping in sweat, Chelsea tried starting the car for some much-needed AC, but the engine refused to turn over. Then, no noise at all. No air. Choking hot.

Desperate to cool down, Chelsea opened the door to step out into the night air that surely mustbe cool by now, but as soon as the door was unlatched, it was ripped from her hands.

Into an abyss, Chelsea is dragged, flailing and screaming, knowing no one will come. Choking on more hot air until-

Chelsea jerked awake, swinging at anything and everything nearby. Twisted in her sheet like a pretzel, it took her nearly falling out of the motel bed to realize she was not in that parking lot, not in that car, not meeting Cooper.

The previous night was filled with what one could describe as pretty boring eavesdropping. Men acting macho, talking about sports, women, work, more women. It was nearly unbearable. The only person who left the house at all was Austin. She followed him to a nearby café and took some pictures of his date but didn't bother following them to the small house.

Austin wasn't high enough on Chelsea's suspect list to bother following more.

About two hours after Austin left and everyone else at the big house, Chelsea thought it finally safe to seek refuge at a nearby, non-horror-movie motel and write down more of her observations. She also wrote down a plan of attack.

That took less time than Chelsea expected, and after those five minutes passed, the rest of the night was filled with channel surfing and unfruitful real estate searching. What Chelsea wanted to do, like most nights away, was call and hear Lexi's voice. Like most nights out, she took a dose of melatonin and fell asleep to whatever was playing on the television. It must have been something suspenseful to magnify her dream like that.

The bedside clock showed a most ungodly hour. At this hour, no one was expected to be awake, let alone moving around. But Chelsea couldn't fall back asleep after what she had just experienced, so she decided to put her extra time to good use.

Chelsea had enough time to try on a new look: a medium-length auburn colored wig, an extra padded push-up bra, and green color contacts.

Chelsea had always wanted to look like that in real life. Alas, it was not to be so. If she *did* have those natural looks, she also couldn't be a spy. It was much too attention-grabbing. So, along with her lack of Irish heritage and the wonderful accent that came with it, Chelsea was stuck with the physical features she currently possessed.

After a final readjustment in the hotel mirror and a snack re-load at the nearest convenience store, Chelsea found herself outside an auction house, waiting for Cooper and Austin to appear.

This was the last job on the Back Road Boy's itinerary, and Cooper said himself that he and Austin would be the ones to handle it.

Chelsea knew who she was looking for but had never seen the two men working together before. As she saw them approach, she thought they looked like it was take-your-child-to-work day. Cooper looked like a corporate father, over-dominating in his cutting-edge suit, no-nonsense demeanor, and such high self-confidence it oozed from every orifice. Meanwhile, Austin, in his ill-fitted business suit, slightly slumped posture, and arms full of a laptop and paperwork, looked more like an older yet childish assistant than a coworker.

Austin's lack of a limp and overall fashion choices told Chelsea he was not the car-tracking mystery man in white shoes. Chelsea mentally crossed him off that list. But it was all for the best because, unknown to Austin, he was about to help Chelsea in a big way.

Chelsea tried to think of what could crack Cooper's superiority complex all morning. What would throw him off track so badly that he would make a mistake? That's when Chelsea wondered, what would happen if one of Cooper's underlings were to "outgirl" him? So, Chelsea decided to cause a bit of a competition between the alpha dog Cooper and the underdog Austin.

Changing her accent along with her appearance, Chelsea could hardly recognize herself, so she wasn't worried about Cooper recognizing her. Chelsea purposefully dressed to kill in snug jeans and a low-cut black shirt that complimented her new bra and wig.

Did Chelsea want to outshine the memory of Tina Bennet and Austin's woman from last night? ....no, not really. But, come on, it was red hair, green eyes, and a stuffed shirt. Who wouldn't fall for that?

It was a difficult decision, but Chelsea chose to stay outside instead of going into the auction house and serving as a distraction. She didn't want to interrupt anybody's work.

While waiting, Chelsea did some general research on what was to be auctioned today. She also looked up some online photos for a good general building layout. She didn't want to be asked why she was inside and not have a good answer.

That didn't take very long. After the first forty-five minutes of waiting, Chelsea still had enough time to try and fail at four easy sudoku puzzles, listen to a talk show about the importance of small talk, and people-watch. If Chelsea wasn't stuck doing this unwanted job, there were three other individuals she would be interested in following. Chelsea was sure she could find some dirt on at least one.

Chapter 24

Cooper and Austin walked out of the auction house just as Chelsea's stomach let out another cry for food. It had been four hours since they walked inside, and Chelsea was just about to reach for one of the snacks she was saving for later.

She would have easily devoured them all by now, but Chelsea needed to invite herself to lunch with her suspects *and* be hungry enough to eat. That's harder than most people expect, especially if you lose your lunch when feeling overwhelmed or uncomfortable.

As soon as Chelsea saw the first person walk out of the auction house, she exited her car and quickly entered the building. She needed to see which numbers won some of the higher-priced items.

Bidder 304 looked favorable, and it didn't matter who used the number because she wasn't going to play the part of the bidder; she was playing a family representative who placed the high-priced items for sale.

All Chelsea needed was for Cooper and Austin to show up and play her little game. Slinking back outside and putting her phone on mute to save potential embarrassment, Chelsea waited on the other side of the door for the two men to walk out. She followed close behind them and spoke loud enough for them to hear.

"Of course, you hoped to come out with more, but auction houses can be unpredictable. The buyer comes out on top, not the seller." Chelsea paused for an adequate amount of time to let her imaginary client respond well. "Don't forget, there is also next week's lot and the cars will do better than the furniture and art pieces. They are in perfect condition."

That was the clincher. Just watching the two men in front of her exchange looks told her she hooked them. Now, to reel them in. "Alright, Dahlia, I'll be in touch. Bye-bye."

Chelsea sighed a little too dramatically and stopped following them to "look around" for her car. As if on cue, Cooper turned around and backtracked to introduce himself. While still looking away, Chelsea took another step to nearly run into Cooper. The accident would give them both an excuse to ease into a conversation.

That Cooper was taken with her getup was unmistakable. Austin at least had the decency not to look her up and down in an obvious way. It was no surprise that Cooper made the first move.

Putting his hands in a spot that guaranteed Chelsea would not walk into him again, Cooper chuckled and smoothly said, "Excuse me, I didn't see you there. Miss…?"

Chelsea took a shocked step back, looked at Cooper, and smiled at Austin. Keeping eye contact with Austin, Chelsea answered, "Carmichael. Emilia Carmichael." Austin just stood there and said nothing.

Cooper, who wanted to keep the conversation going, stepped slightly closer and in front of Austin. Chelsea knew that was both an Alpha move as well as an insecure one, but Cooper just put on a smile and asked, "Miss Carmichael. My associate and I couldn't help but overhear you have some cars up for auction?"

"Well, I sure hope you overheard," Miss Carmichael answered Cooper, then turned her gaze back to Austin, "Or else I wouldn't have said it so loud."

She liked the confused looks on both their faces, mostly because they were genuine and partly because they gave her a power trip. It was finally time to play the player.

Motioning back towards the auction house, Miss Carmichael explained. "I noticed you two inside. I also noticed you were bidding on vehicles, so I'm glad I could catch up with you during my phone call. I'd love to talk with you about my employer's pristine cars, but I'm much more pleasant to speak with on a full stomach. That is if you two don't have anything going on right now and could accompany me to an early dinner?"

Knowing it would aggravate him even more, Chelsea only addressed Austin while asking them to dinner. Seeing Cooper uncomfortable was more satisfying than seeing him confused.

"I'm sorry, I never asked for your name, and here I am asking you to dinner. You are?" Again, Cooper took the initiative with introductions, but Chelsea waited for Austin to confirm before continuing.

Chelsea finally offered Cooper a smile to keep his interest. "Well, gentlemen, I know a great restaurant just down the street. Meet me there, and I'll happily share *anything* you'd like to know."

It was good that Chelsea knew quite a bit about cars from working with her uncle a few years back. She had the men practically drooling over the fictional luxury vehicles. But when she said the owners would be unable to show them until next week, the desire to own the cars faded, and the desire to possess *her* grew.

Their dinner location was nearby and nearly empty, with a full bar stationed along the back wall. Once seated, Chelsea strategically placed herself next to Austin instead of Cooper, hoping to goad him even more. As Chelsea expected, Cooper quietly excused himself to the bar after realizing he wouldn't get what he wanted.

Cooper's leaving gave Austin too much confidence. After all the attention Chelsea gave Austin, she found it necessary to not just tap the breaks on things as soon as they were alone but slam on them.

Chelsea leaned in and, quietly so no one overheard them, asked, "Tell me, is he always like that? Pouty and irritable when being ignored?" Austin leaned in, too, much too close for Chelsea's comfort. "Cooper, yes. Me? Try to ignore me all you want. I'm not going anywhere." Even though she was severely uncomfortable with their physical proximity, Chelsea didn't look away. Instead, as seductively as possible, she asked, "And what would your wife and kids think about that?" "Huh?" Austin withdrew his face at whiplash speed.

Chelsea didn't give him time to do anything else before explaining, "The tan line on your finger. I'm not blind. And I happened to look you up."

The look on his face was indescribable. Chelsea wondered, would he yell, curse, cry? Knowing you're committing adultery is one thing; being caught is another, and he didn't even know how much she knew.

Chelsea scooted closer to Austin to pin him to the wall, dropped the act, and cut to the chase. Chelsea said aggressively, "Austin before you get up and run away, I think you need to hear what I have to say."

Austin didn't seem to take this very well. He looked like he would push Chelsea out of the dining booth until she hastily said, "Not only can this information keep you from a messy divorce, but it may even get you off the FBI's watch list. Is there any way I can trust you not to say anything to Cooper, Jonathan, Kevin, or Zech?""How the hell-!"Chelsea cut him off in an even gruff tone than before, showing she meant business. "Ssshh, stop that right now. This is important, and I reallyneed you to keep it together, okay?"

Looking around in a daze, Austin tried to catch Cooper's eye without calling for him. Chelsea wondered if this decision was the best after all. But hell, these men were leaving late tomorrow morning, and she needed some answers now.

Glancing in Cooper's direction and seeing they were being watched, Chelsea gave Cooper a little wave before turning back to Austin with a most threatening glare. "Look, I need you to reassure your friend over there that everything is okay. If not, I'll call up the wife within five minutes of leaving this place, and you'll never again have to worry about someone covering for you when you take your dates to the tiny house."

"Who the hell are you!" Austin responded with a sort of growling whisper and had Chelsea not been paying full attention to him, she would have misunderstood what he said.

Wiping all looks of aggression from her face and replacing them with a demeanor of authority, Chelsea answered, "I don't think you want to know who I am, Austin Trujillo, so I'm not going to tell you. But I will tell you this. I know you don't want me here any more than I want to be here, so let's make this quick. Yes, I am blackmailing you. No, this probably won't be the only time I'll use your extramarital affairs against you. That being said, you need to decide right now if you're going to help me or bury yourself because, like I said before, I'll call up your wife within five minutes of leaving if you don't."

Austin sat in stunned silence, then turned to stare at his half-eaten plate in front of him. After thirty seconds, Chelsea couldn't take it any longer. "Tick tock, Austin."

"What do you want? And what do you mean by FBI's watch list?" He was hurt, scared, furious, and Chelsea couldn't blame him one bit. Didn't she feel the same when Chief practically blackmailed her?

"I want your help." It surprised her a little that Austin, of all people, was the person she chose to turn to for help. But she couldn't dwell on that right now. Instead, she asked, "Do any of these names and places sound familiar?"

Chelsea started with the most recent victim's name and location and went backward. It wasn't until she was on the third name that Austin visually paled, and by the seventh, he looked like he was going to throw up.

"Yeah, yeah, I've heard their names. Those were all Cooper's girls, though, none of mine. You can't tell my wife I had anything to do with them!" The underlying panic in his voice told Chelsea he was telling the truth. And he didn't have much to gain from lying to her anyway.

Chelsea felt a little reassurance could go a long way to get him on her side, so she loosened up and sat back, facing the table. "I don't plan on telling your wife anything about them. I just needed to confirm you knew who they were." Pausing a little to ensure she worded it right, Chelsea asked, "Are you sure they were all Cooper's girls? *Only* Cooper's?" A little too quickly, Austin confirmed, "Yes, and if any of them say they were with me, they're lying.""Well," Chelsea finally turned back to look Austin in the eye before continuing, "seeing as they're all dead, I don't think that will be a problem."

Both were stunned silent. Chelsea didn't exactly plan on telling Austin *that* much information, so much for the cat staying in the bag. A small, chaotic storm ensued in that little booth.

"Omigod. Omigod!"

"Austin, keep it together.""Omigod!""Austin!"

Chelsea yell-whispered at him. "Cooper doesn't know. At least, I hope he doesn't. But if he's as aggressive as you say, was the only person to have physically been with those women *and* found out, *you know*! Well, I'm not exactly sure what he'd do in that situation, buddy, so pull it together and calm the frick down!"

Austin's eyes shot to the bar, and Chelsea's followed. Cooper was gone, and neither knew where. "Where did he go!?" was their unanimous blurt. The bar that was nearly empty when they arrived had quite a few patrons now, and when the crowd moved slightly, they could see Cooper on the other side talking with a well-endowed woman wearing too little clothing.

Dyed hair, heavy makeup, and gawdy clothing…this woman made Chelsea feel slightly offended. After all, Cooper did leave Chelsea's company to talk with…that. But Chelsea couldn't let her personal feelings get in the way now. She needed to get back to blackmailing Austin.

Austin looked like he was going to have a heart attack. Backing ever so slightly away from this sweaty, panting mess, Chelsea handed Austin her napkin and said, "I am not implicating any which way as to whether Cooper did something to these women. Just because they are no longer alive does not make *him* the killer. I just want to know a few things about him. So, will you help me, or do I need to make a phone call?"

"No, no, I'll help you." Austin still looked a little worse for wear. But Chelsea didn't fault him for that. All of this would have been a shock for anyone. And he did just hear of seven women being murdered. There was no reason to tell him about the other six or more victims.

"Thank you." It was a relief for Chelsea to feel like someone was finally on her side, and she was sincere in her gratitude. Thinking now was as good a time as ever, Chelsea asked Austin her first question. "Will you please tell me if any of you have new or pristine white tennis shoes?"

"White shoes, are you serious? What does that have to do with anything!" It was an odd question, but he didn't need to look at her like she was stupid.

"Please, just answer the question." It was easier for her to be polite the first time she asked. Chelsea hoped he didn't make her ask him a third time.

With a little attitude, Austin scoffed, "About whether or not we wear shoes, yeah. But I don't care about shoes, so they could be wearing red heels for all I know. ""Okay, that's fine." Chelsea wanted to start nice, but his sudden change in attitude upset her. Time to go for the jugular. "Do you always rent two houses instead of staying at the hotel during your work trips?"

Austin was a little more hesitant in answering this one. "Austin?""Yes. Yes, we do.""Every time?""Yes."

Okay, she thought. *Now we're getting somewhere.*

"Do you all take a turn at the second house?" Austin's silence was answer enough. Chelsea continued. "Every trip? Or is it mostly Cooper and the occasional someone else who gets that privilege?"

"We usually all get a chance to use it, all of us but Zech. He's *'got convictions'*. It doesn't keep him from covering for us, though. Any time we're, well, preoccupied, he'll answer our phone if someone calls."

Chelsea prayed Austin didn't know she had a connection with Zech. She was pleased to hear he didn't partake in those activities but to coverfor them… that made him a willing accomplice, and Chelsea didn't know how she felt about that.

Mistaking Chelsea's silence and her stunned look, Austin hastily went on. "Cooper uses the second house the most, though. Always first, always the most."

Not looking at Austin anymore and bogged down by other thoughts, it was a little time before Chelsea asked, "Was it Cooper's idea to get the second houses in the first place?""Yes," Austin answered without hesitation, "He thought bringing women over to a house full of guys would be too intimidating to do…well…you know?"

"Unfortunately, I do."

Knowing their remaining time was short, Chelsea took another glance in Cooper's direction to make sure he was still preoccupied. Satisfied and unsatisfied with what she saw, Chelsea looked back at Austin and asked, "Are there any set rules other than Cooper goes first and not to let anybody else find out?"

"Yeah," Austin shrugged and answered, "Never see the same girl twice."

Never twice? An internal siren went off in Chelsea's head. That was suspicious, but Cooper hadn't been a model citizen for following the rules even if he was the one who set them.

"Why not?" Chelsea continued. "Why would that be such a bad idea?""Well," Austin grabbed his water glass and took a long drink. At first, it looked like he was thinking of an excuse to give, but then he answered, and Chelsea thought he must have just been very thirsty.

"It makes them feel like they can come back whenever. And if they ever found someone else at the house with another woman or the same guy with a different one, ...it's easier to have a one-time-only policy."

That made too much sense. So why would Cooper risk such a thing with a woman as volatile as Valerie? "Could you meet them more than once outside the house?"Austin chuckled at what he thought was a stupid question. "Well, I guess. But if you couldn't bring them home, then why would you?"

Chelsea's glare made him physically recoil. There was at least one reason someone would meet those thirteen women in the file sitting on her passenger seat.

Weighing her desire for more information against her distaste for this man, Chelsea finally relinquished her curiosity. "Thank you, Austin. That will be all for now."

. Chelsea began to slide out of her seat, indicating their conversation was finished. "Wait, are you serious!? You can't leave me alone with him!"

Chelsea stopped because of Austin's panic-stricken voice. Turning her head in his direction but unwilling to make eye contact, Chelsea countered, "Well, you hide extra relationships from your wife all the time. Now you get to hide one conversation from your buddies, especially Cooper."

That didn't do much to assuage his fear. "But what if he finds out about this? And that I know? What if he *did* kill them, and he kills me too!?"

Finally looking Austin in the eye, Chelsea gestured for him to keep his voice down and whispered, "As I said, there is no proof Cooper killed them. I just needed more information."

"And I drew the short stick?" Austin asked curtly."...something like that, yes.""You bi-"Chelsea cut him off, "Again, yes."

A silent, heated minute passed between the two of them. Austin was practically stabbing Chelsea with his eyes. Chelsea gave a conceded sigh and pulled a pen from her purse.

Taking a different, non-sweaty napkin from the table, Chelsea quickly wrote a phone number down and slid it over to Austin. "Here. If you have *any* suspicions of being in danger, or Cooper knows, or anything, call this number. It will get you in touch with the Tulsa chief of police. Tell him a Miss Jordan Chief gave this to you, and you're aiding in her investigation. He'll know what to do. And for what I hope are obvious reasons, don't tell anyone else we spoke."

Austin stared at the napkin, reached for it with a shaking hand, and then drew it back as if he feared that touching it would put him in more danger. If Chelsea didn't find him to be a completely disgusting person, she would feel a little sorry watching his hands shake.

Licking his lips, Austin took a few tentative breaths before looking at Chelsea. "I'm reallythe only person who knows about this? This isn't some prank or something from the guys?"

Feeling a pang of sorrow for him despite herself, Chelsea sighed and confirmed his unfortunate position. "Yes, you are. And no, it's not. I wish so much that it was." Hesitating, unsure if she was doing the right thing, Chelsea whispered, "Please, Austin, say nothing to no one," before slipping out of the booth.

Choosing to slip was a bad idea. As soon as Chelsea stood up, she had to reposition her outfit. It was amazing how sitting can shift clothing, let alone sliding across a faux leather booth.

Shoving the phone number in his pocket, Austin picked up another napkin to wipe his brow. "Don't worry, I plan on going to the house, downing some drinks, and going straight to bed. Then it's home to look for another job.""Sounds like a good idea to me. Have a good night. I'll be in touch." And with that, Chelsea bee-lined for the door. She didn't even bother to see if Cooper was watching her.

Chapter 25

Chelsea was only two steps outside the restaurant when she realized she never told Austin *how* she would keep in touch. That could account for his terrified look as she turned to leave, but the situation was already scary enough, so her little blunder couldn't take all the credit.

Pulling into a gas station two stores down with a change of clothes, Chelsea changed out of her outfit and wig in the surprisingly clean restroom. The look on the attendant's face would have made her laugh if she wasn't in such a vulnerable situation. She was banking everything on whether a perpetual cheater could keep a secret from a domineering, possible serial killer.

Chelsea walked back to the restaurant's parking lot and waited. Watching the two men leave the restaurant and how they interacted with each other would tell her a lot.

The two men were bantering back and forth without any look of fear or discomfort on either of their faces. Cooper seemed easy to forgive, and Austin seemed easy to please. All was normal, and that gave Chelsea a little reassurance.

Chelsea didn't have to follow them to know they drove straight home. She watched the little dot on her phone travel the familiar streets to its intended location. Another dot was at the tiny house.

Chelsea thought about driving to the tiny house, but knowing enough of what was going on there, decided it was unnecessary.

Instead, Chelsea drove to a different trailhead that led to the Back Road Boy's backyard. Once the cover of darkness came, she positioned herself in the neighbor's backyard.

The front of the neighbor's house gave the impression they were out of town, and the back confirmed it. This was a relief. It was best not to park out on the road anymore. Not after hearing Zech was home the whole time and unsure if he saw her.

Staying on the back porch but still of sight, Chelsea sat as comfortably as possible and listened through her earpiece. Chelsea had to check her surroundings frequently to see if any creepy crawlies snuck up on her, but that was just part of the job.

True to his word, Austin started downing drinks with the others as soon as he got home. From what she could decipher, it seemed everyone was ready for a fun night, minus Jonathan… His poor fiancée needed to get far away from this mess.

Had Chelsea thought of it sooner, she would have taken pictures of the man and posted them on his social media account for the world to see. Or at least privately messaged them to his fiancée. But Jonathan was a cyber genius, and Chelsea… not so much. Besides, this was going to be Chelsea's last job. It had to be.

Some jeering brought Chelsea's mind back to the present. Austin seemed to have downed too many drinks at record pace and excused himself for the night. This provoked the others, calling his stomach as weak as Zech's.

A light turned on upstairs, emitting a soft yellow glow through the curtains. It was no good trying to reach him there. She had a hard enough time getting in and out through a downstairs window. This meant, should Chelsea ever need to reach Austin, it would have to be while he was out and about.

Some more jeering caught Chelsea's ears, and she turned her focus back to the remaining guys.

"…but Austin? I mean, come on. I was standing right there." Cooper's voice sounded less bitter and more humorous than she expected. She was sure he would have been upset.

"Hey, we all have off days. Maybe your mojo isn't as good as you think it is." Chelsea huffed. This was rich, coming from Kevin. But then again, he was riding a high from that morning, and it would take more than Cooper's disapproval to wipe the smug look off his face.

At least, Chelsea assumed he had a smug look. It sounded like he did over the earpiece.

Zech interrupted what sounded like some shoving going on in the background. "Can we talk about something else, please? Like, what we're doing tomorrow?"

Yes, Chelsea thought, *let's talk about that.*

"We have all the usual things to wrap up before leaving," Cooper said. "You know that."

Chelsea held her breath, waiting for specifics.

Kevin groaned slightly before saying, "Jonathan said he'd wrap things up at the other place since he's there already. So, let me guess. *I* clean this house while you and three finish some jobs."

"You and Austin can clean things up here, and Jonathan is going to finish all the paperwork for the auction house," Cooper answered. Pausing long enough to take a drink, Cooper continued. "Zech and I have other things to do."

"Like what?" Zech asked.

Chelsea's heartbeat began to roar in her ears. She needed to stop holding her breath.

"Well," Cooper answered Zech a little harsher than necessary, "You haven't done anything all damn week, and I'm tired of you being such a useless git."

"Useless?" Zech didn't sound like he was asking as much as accusing. "I work plenty hard for this team, even if I'm not on the streets. Don't go forgetting that."

"Enough," Kevin interjected. "What are you two up to?"

Both tried to answer, but Cooper talked over Zech. "Zech here has a last-minute deal to handle. And since he's finally feeling better, I pushed that one off to him."

"And you?" Zech asked.

"Bank run. Unless *you'd* rather personally finance our out-of-town entertainment?" There was no audible answer, and Cooper continued, "If you finish early, let me know, and I'll add the transactions to the ledgers. Don't forget, we must get to the airport early."

Chelsea couldn't believe they were leaving tomorrow morning. Chelsea scampered out of the backyard and slowly went to the hiking trail. She had her black light on the whole time to make sure no unpleasant night critters were about. Once she was sure no one would see the light, Chelsea pulled out Valerie's phone and quickly began typing.

Are we still on for tomorrow morning? I have something I think you might like.

There was an uncomfortably long wait before Chelsea realized Cooper wasn't going to answer her. She had to up her game.

Want me to describe it?

Still nothing. Giving him another chance to answer Valerie, Chelsea typed, *Or do you want a picture instead?*

Her questions remained unanswered. Chelsea, or rather, Valerie, had just been ghosted.

Pulling out her other phone, Chelsea dialed another number. Voicemail. It wasn't the first time she wished her rule was broken, just once, but there was nothing she could do about it now.

"Chief? Cooper's a scumbag, alright, but I trailed him all week and nothing. He either isn't the guy or decided to break the routine on this trip for some reason. I'll give you more details in the office….. And…sorry for not coming home when I first said I was, but a deal is a deal, and I will hold you to it."

Chelsea hung up. Walking down the trail, she was unsure how she felt now that the case was over. Was she thankful not to have flirted with a serial murderer? Yes. No doubt about that. But this left one very uneasy thought in Chelsea's mind. Whoever the killer was was still out there. And so was her Mystery Man.

Chapter 26

Chelsea had been sitting at the airport for twenty minutes, watching the Back Road Boys from two gates away. She wasn't sure what new information she would find here, but her job wasn't technically done until they reached Tulsa. Well, that was half her reason. Surveying the group also allowed Chelsea to write off a much-deserved, overpriced, frozen coffee beverage.

Sitting there with her eyes on the men and her mind wandering, Chelsea realized she still needed to pick up a gift for Lexi. Finding something without the state's flag, name, symbol, or sports team on it would prove difficult, but Chelsea was confident she would find something.

Chelsea started making her way to the nearest gift shop when a man with a slight limp and obnoxiously white shoes caught the corner of her eye. And he was not alone.

Chelsea's instincts immediately kicked in. Beelining for the nearest crowd, she skirted the group while always keeping her eye on him. Watching her mystery man come ever closer, flanked by two others on each side, Chelsea began to take some mental notes.

It was obvious they were not fliers, not the way they were walking or how they held themselves. Four men, one woman. Outside two scanning the crowd for…?

A chill ran up her spine. She sat down facing away and used a reflective glass to watch the group pass her. The outside two were looking for someone, and she hoped it wasn't her.

Once they passed, Chelsea saw they were flocking to the Back Road Boy's gate. Fanning out as soon as they arrived, Chelsea saw them reach for their sidearms as her mystery man yelled, "Cooper Gray, FBI! Drop everything and lay down with your hands on your head, Now!"

The other four were making similar commands of Jonathan, Austin, Zech, and Kevin.

What happened next shocked Chelsea.

It was understandable for Cooper to be confused and take longer than expected to respond. What was not understandable was Cooper getting tackled to comply with their demands.

Shocked voices were everywhere, and the crowds closed in despite the orders to stand back and move aside.

Chelsea heard Cooper yelling out questions and a few choice words, claiming he had no idea what they wanted when an agent Chelsea had not noticed was suddenly at her side.

"Chelsea Markwell?"

Hearing her name made Chelsea jump so violently that the rest of her coffee was lost on the floor.

A female agent not much older than herself waited for Chelsea to regain composure before she asked Chelsea to follow her to a more secluded area.

Looking back to the Back Road Boys, Chelsea saw Jonathan, Zech, and Kevin were in an uproar, firing off questions and throwing up their hands in innocence at whatever their boss had done. On the other hand, Austin looked as if he would throw up any second. He had not moved or said a word since seeing his boss being tackled to the ground.

"Miss Markwell!" the urgency in the female agent's voice was unmistakable. "I understand you have a flight back to Tulsa, and I promise to make sure you get there on time. However, I have a few questions for you…off the record."

"That sounds like something you say before making someone disappear." Chelsea hated hearing the fear in her voice.

Giving an obvious smirk, the agent's cold eyes didn't reassure Chelsea. Then she said, "Think of it as a professional courtesy. You prefer to hide in plain sight and blend into the shadows, so asking you to come quietly should have been appreciated. Or would you rather I yell your name and tackle you, too?"

Looking back again, Chelsea noted the crowd thinning from flights needing to be made. She also saw several photos and videos being made and decided to take the woman up on her offer to go with her quietly.

Chelsea was led to the corner of an empty gate. The woman sat in one set of sectioned chairs and waited for Chelsea to do likewise. The seat was still warm from the last person to occupy it, but the metal armrests were freezing, and the mixed temperatures made Chelsea even more uneasy. Chelsea looked around for the nearest trash can.

While surveying the area just in case, Chelsea wasn't paying attention when the woman said, "You gave us quite the run-around, Mrs. Markwell." That caught Chelsea's attention and kept it.

Confused and quite disappointed in herself for not noticing when *she* was being watched, Chelsea couldn't help herself from asking. "I did?"

Taking care to fold her hands so as not to fidget, crossing her ankles to not bob her knees, and looking Chelsea straight in the eye, the agent leaned forward, wanting no question about who was in charge.

Body language can tell you a lot about a person, and what Chelsea saw next told her this mystery agent was a no-nonsense person with a dominant attitude. Chelsea didn't exactly like the woman, but there was no way she, or anybody else, would disrespect her.

With a cold voice to match her cold gaze, the agent answered, "Yes, Mrs. Markwell, you did," and sat back in her seat.

"When my agent put the tracking device on Miss Morana's car, only to be stolen by you, I was quite miffed. Too often, this man has harmed another human being, and by your actions, it looked like *you* were helping him. So, we tagged your car instead during that little fiasco in front of the house."

"You were lucky we didn't arrest you after we saw you followed Miss Morana home. Or when you stole her phone."

Chelsea shifted uncomfortably in her chair. From the outside, it did look like she was the bad guy.

"But," the agent continued, "thanks to some *extensive* research on our end, we were finally able to find out who you were and what you were doing."

Chelsea was not known to blush, but she couldn't help it. It was also difficult for Chelsea to tell if this was a reprimand or a praise. So as not to upset the agent, Chelsea sat in her chair, silent, and nodded in understanding.

That was good enough for the agent, and she continued speaking. "We contacted your police chief. He admitted to putting you on the case *despite* our suggestion not to hinder or interfere." Taking a pause, the woman composed her thoughts before asking, "He seems to think you have some evidence to exonerate Mr. Gray from the murder of Miss Morana as well as the past victims?"

"Yes, you see, he just…doesn't… Hold on, did you say the *murder* of Miss *Morana?!*" Chelsea talked before fully understanding what was said.

The agent finally broke character. "Yes. My agents found her in her house this morning same MO as the others, all except the body's location. She was not buried at an offsite location. That, I assume, was mostly due to lack of time, but that is still speculation."

Chelsea couldn't believe her ears. Valerie was murdered?

There was something else bothering Chelsea. "But…there's so much that doesn't make sense. How did he even know where she lived?"

The mystery agent stood, signaling they were done speaking. "That information, I intend to extract from him myself. I only came here to warn you: Stay. Away. From MY cases. You are *not* an FBI agent, and we will not stand for *any* more meddling from a lowly private 'detective' like you. Do you understand?"

The woman's tone was an intimidating low, like the guttural growl of a wolf, and Chelsea heard the threat in it. Chelsea was off the case whether Chief said so or not, and she was commanded not to speak about it to anyone. But things still didn't sound right.

"But," Chelsea continued, despite knowing better, "when would he have done it? I followed Cooper the whole time, except for this morning, but he was only going to the bank."

The agent scoffed. "Not the whole time. Morana's phone records will prove your laziness. Now, excuse me, I have a murderer to book."

And with that, the woman left Chelsea with many thoughts. Sadly, none of them were about her daughter's forgotten present. Only when she was boarded and nursing a headache did she remember Lexi still needed something to make up for her mother's absence.

Chapter 27

"I told you, Chelsea. I don't want to hear any more of your 'buts' on this! If you have *anything* useful to defend him, get in touch with his lawyers and pass that information off to them. As of now, we are done."

The day after coming home, Chelsea was standing in Chief Jordan's office. He had dismissed Chelsea from duty yesterday and said she was free to go, but Chelsea couldn't help it. Something was off. "Cooper did nothing wrong!"

Chief's eyebrows rose skeptically.

"Okay, he did a *ton* of things wrong, but he didn't murder her!" Chelsea had been trying in vain for the last twenty minutes to get Chief to listen to her.

"And you know that for a fact?"

"Yes!"

His eyebrows rose again.

"Yes, in a sense, yes, I do! The agent mentioned phone records between Cooper and Morana, but there *couldn't* have been phone records between Cooper and Morana because *I* had her phone!"

"You, what?"

"Yeah! I stole it after thinking she would tell Cooper who I was. So, he was talking to *me,* not her. And *I'm* still alive. So… who was Valerie actually talking to?"

Chief shook his head in anger. "Chelsea, are you some kind of special stupid or something?!"

"Huh?"

"You just admitted to a police chief that you stole someone else's property. Someone who is now *dead by the way*. And you think, because there's *No Way* she could get another phone in, oh, I don't know, an Hour, that *That's* proof to go against a scary FBI woman!?"

"Well, when you put it that way."

"Damn, Chelsea! You were supposed to get in, get the evidence, and get out. It was so straightforward!"

That was the first time she heard someone yell her name like that in years, and it brought back so many painful memories. Memories that couldn't be kept behind her eyelids.

Frantically wiping her eyes, Chelsea stood and left the office without another word. If she were going to get any help, it wouldn't be from Chief.

Passing by Joe's desk on her way out of the precinct, Chelsea saw Joe wasn't there. She called Joe last night after Lexi went to bed, and his reaction was similar but nicer than the Chief's just now. Maybe it was for the best he wasn't there. She didn't want to be let down by him, too.

There was also something going on with Joe that he wasn't telling her about, and it would just be selfish to press him into helping with her botched investigation.

Until now, there were only two cases Chelsea had a difficult time letting go. Two out of at least a hundred. But this one?

It had been three days since Chelsea arrived home, and despite popular belief, she could not stomach thinking Cooper was a killer. What made things worse was hearing her sister and brother-in-law talk about it constantly while she could not contribute to the conversation other than feigned shock, disbelief, and a well-placed question. Chelsea had to stick to her story of exposing an MLM real estate scam.

All the news channels and social media were carrying on about Cooper and his associates, making it difficult to say anything against the wave of haters. There was only one person Chelsea felt she could talk with, but there was a problem there, too.

Joe wouldn't speak with her. Chelsea still didn't know what was wrong with him, but every time she reached out to have a cup of joe with her Joe, there was one reason or another for him not to meet her. After years of friendship, she knew that wasn't a coincidence.

No matter, Chelsea thought, *he doesn't have to speak with me if he doesn't want to.*

But today had been a long day, and it was only noon.

Chelsea contemplated going by Lexi's school for lunch but couldn't stomach anything now, especially not cafeteria food. And last time she was there, it was over-crowded, and hygiene protocols were anything but followed.

After getting a coffee anyway and hoping Joe would show up at their park, Chelsea spent two hours on a bench, mentally reviewing everything again.

Two hours and Chelsea had nothing. She was ready to call it a day and go home but needed to get her mail at her sister's place first. She tried to avoid their house until the curious and unwanted paparazzi disappeared.

"Hey, Miriam? Miriam, I'm here to get my mail." Chelsea rarely knocked when she visited her sister, but she was courteous enough to announce her presence. "Miriam?"

Looking and listening told her the house was empty; a sticky note on the counter beside her mail confirmed it. Today was soccer practice for all the kids, and Miriam ran out to get refreshments for everyone. "*Including You*" was written, letting Chelsea know she was not excused from attending. It seemed Chesea would be heading to the soccer field instead of her bed after all.

Next to her mail, Chelsea noticed a small, half-unpacked gift for her sister. It was a sweet thing Zech did, getting a gift for Miriam every time he went away. It's also what started Chelsea's habit of buying Lexi a keepsake. A habit that was only broken this time, with no proper excuse to give. This made her crappy day even worse.

Chelsea made a mental note. *Soccer practice, then gift shopping; check.*

Chelsea had no reason to look in the box. Maybe it was curiosity, maybe it was to get her gift idea for Lexi, or maybe, just maybe, it was that nagging voice in her head telling her to look at the details. When did Zech ever have time to get Miriam a gift on his trip?

There was packing tissue in excess. Chelsea expected to feel the cool, hard texture of glass or metal. Something to explain the overpacking. Instead, what she felt was made of cotton and velvet. No, not velvet, feathers.

An intricate purple dream catcher with brown and white feathers, identical to the one in Valerie Morana's car, sat in Chelsea's shaking hands.

Bile rose in her throat. Either someone was playing a sick joke on her, or she was about to be on the wrong end of a horror story. With her hands still shaking, she looked closer at the box. It was unmistakably Zech's handwriting but the box wasn't addressed to Miriam. It was addressed to Chelsea.

Chelsea bent over the kitchen sink and purged. She didn't even hear the front door open or sense someone entering the room. She could only think about the dreamcatcher lying on the counter next to her. Then, she was grabbed.

Only one other time before was Chelsea physically assaulted on a job, and that was with her consent. Sure, Chelsea could throw a punch and kick in the right places, but that was when she was aware of the danger and facing her assailant. This caught her completely off guard.

A towel covered Chelsea's mouth so she couldn't scream or bite. Her arms were pinned to her side by someone much stronger, and she was bent back so she couldn't get her legs behind her and kick him. Him, for it was obvious that a man was attacking her. Chelsea tried to kick off the kitchen cabinets to throw her attacker off balance, but he was too quick and smart.

Chelsea was dragged backward towards the front of the house, but instead of heading to the door, she was dragged left towards the stairs. He dragged her five steps up, then shoved her down. Chelsea didn't even register pain before all thoughts and senses turned to black.

Chapter 28

The first thing Chelsea felt was the pain in her left cheek. That must have been where she hit the wall first. The second thing she realized was her legs and hands were free from any restraints.

Her eyes fluttered open, and the initial light was blinding. So much so it was hard for Chelsea to recognize her whereaboutsThen, to her horror, she realized the carpet she was recently face down onwas familiar.

"I played you from the start, *Cece*." The calm voice sent ice shooting through Chelsea's veins. No matter what she *knew*, Chelsea still couldn't comprehend what was happening. Then, her eyes adjusted to the dream catcher dangling from her brother-in-law's hand.

Chelsea saw Zech sitting on the edge of his bed, strategically between her and the bedroom door. The door to their bathroom was on the other side of the bed, along with the only window in the room. Zech couldn't have picked a better place to hold Chelsea. He knew that. He planned it.

Chelsea coughed a response to Zech as she tried to sit up more, but her head was spinning too hard to move much.

"I didn't catch that, Cece. What did you say?" He was mocking her, but there wasn't any way for him to know what she said.

Panting from her spinning head and threatening stomach, Chelsea spays out. "Don't *call* me that."

Zech cocked his head, narrowed his eyes at her, and said, "No, I think I will, *Cece*. And I don't think you'll do a thing about it."

Zech chuckled as Chelsea took stock of her injuries. She noticed her right ankle was hurting, but not nearly as much as her left shoulder. Unfortunately, Chelsea knew that unless she got away from here, away from *him*, these injuries would be found moot.

Chelsea studied those files, the women in them. She knew their killer was meticulous, domineering, preyed upon them and likely their fears, and Chelsea was not going to give Zech the satisfaction of getting a rise out of her. Not while she could help it.

In as strong and calm a voice as she could muster, Chelsea shrugged her good shoulder and said, "Fine, call me Cece. I don't care."

Zech could see the determination in her eyes. He'd seen it before and knew how to break her. Leaning forward, Zech smirked and said, "Oh, I think you care, *Cece*, but you go ahead and tell yourself otherwise. You wouldn't be the first." He tossed the dream catcher toward her, and Chelsea flinched away.

Finally, Zech was ready to do something he had waited long to do. Something he knew was going to destroy her and make her his forever. Zech was finally going to tell Chelsea the truth.

Leaning back, Zech recalled with fondness, "I messed with you the whole week, and it was so much fun." Chelsea was giving quick, short shakes with her head as if she didn't want to hear him but couldn't help it.

Waiting a few seconds but continuing when Chelsea said nothing, Zech added, "I knew you were outside the house that first night. And I made sure you heard everything I wanted you to. I also knew you were in my room, and you went to Cooper's afterward."

Chelsea tried to regroup. I tried to fidget or look bored. Anything to make it seem as if she didn't care what he had to say. But all Chelsea could do was say, "No, no, no." over and over while her head kept shaking on its own accord.

Pausing, savoring what he was about to say next, Zech leaned forward again, his forearms on his knees, and waited for Chelsea to give him her full attention before saying, "You led me straight to Valerie Morana's house. Thank you for that."

That last statement was what got to her. Finally, the mystery Chelsea had gone over time and time again in her head was solved. Chelsea's eyes bulged, and she couldn't help but take the bait. Panting now, Chelsea cried, "But how? The tracker I took off her car belonged to the FBI."

Smiling at her reaction, Zech shook his head and, most condescendingly, said, "Cece, I never tagged her car; I tagged yours. Or, rather, I tagged Tina Bennet's."

"As soon as I saw you at the resort, I knew something was happening. And it was stupid to rent a car from my own company. Did you not think I would look to see if a Chelsea Markwell or Tina Bennet had rented from one of our nearby locations?"

The truth was, yes. She never once thought he would look up the alias she gave him or look her up to see if the names matched any of their recent customers. She never thought she would have to hide from him.

"It's not difficult to look someone up in the system, Cece. It didn't take more than ten minutes to find your car in the parking lot and put my tracker on it, and I didn't even have to do that stupid tie-the-shoe bit you do."

Chelsea bit back a reply, but it was hard to keep the shock off her face, so Zech kept talking.

"And while you were wiggling your way into Cooper's life, I started setting him up to take my fall for mine."

The pain Chelsea felt then was indescribable. Not once did she suspect Zech or even think him capable of such hideousness. The betrayal cut deep into her bones; betrayal and fear flooded her very being, for if she could be this wrong about a person so close to her, who else did she know with an evil side just waiting to come out and play?

Tears couldn't keep themselves at bay. A vise was gripping her heart. Turning her face away from the pain of betrayal and guilt, it was several seconds until her breathing evened out, and she could speak again. She already knew the answer to her question but had to ask anyway. "You only find her because of me? I'm the reason she's dead?"

"No, Chelsea." The words sounded so sincere, so full of compassion. He even used her real name. "You're not the reason she's dead."

Her head flew back to face him. She was a fool to hope for even a second.

"You're the reason they're *all* dead."

Chapter 29

Chelsea's throat tightened so much she could barely choke out, "Wh-what?"

The smile that tugged at the corner of Zech's mouth could only be described as wicked. "Lindsey Tate of Sapulpa. Remember her?"

Of course, Chelsea remembered her. She was her first and only female infidelity case. The first case she ever needed help with—Zech's help.

Zech rose from the bed and took half a step closer to Chelsea. She instinctively tried to crawl away, but her ankle and shoulder wouldn't allow much movement. Crawling would have also led Chelsea closer to a corner and further from her only exit.

Zech didn't stop closing in on Chelsea until she was cowering in front of him, too afraid to throw up. He crouched down and waited for her to stop squirming before continuing his verbal assault. "I was so happy you asked me to help you with that case. You wanna know why?" He waited for Chelsea to shake her head. "Because I already knew you would make your case. I was the one she was cheating with."

Chelsea continued shaking her head. Silent tears began streaking her face, but she refused to follow along. "No. No, you were the bait. You two never met before."

Zech sighed as if he was disappointed in her and stood up, still careful to block her exit. "This town isn't as big as people make it out to be, Chelsea. And people in Sapulpa need rental cars, too. You get to meet many people behind the desk at a rental car facility."

Chelsea forgot that, back then, he was still working at the local Back Road Rental store. She desperately wanted to refuse the truth Zech was sharing, but that didn't stop him from continuing.

"You want to know the best part about you asking for my help, Chels? You were my way out without anyone being the wiser. Sure, Miriam was fuming and threatened all sorts of things once she knew what I did to help you, but she wasn't nearly as mad as she would have been knowing the truth. And besides, didn't you think it was *too* easy for me to get the evidence we needed?"

She did. She always thought Zech had charisma, but it was all-too-easy to catch Lindsey Tate cheating on her husband. But instead of questioning it, she envied how easy that job was for Zech and began doubting her abilities.

Zech almost relished the memories and what they were doing to Chelsea. Then, out of nowhere, Zech's face went grim, and his voice sounded cold as steel. "After Lindsey was exposed to her husband, she wanted to make it even; tell Miriam. She even went as far as to call her right in front of me, so I stopped her. And it was so, *so* easy to stop her and get away with it. Unlike all the others, I spent a whole week with her, calling in sick and "going to work." And here everyone thought poor Mrs. Tate ran off in shame, hiding from her husband and wicked deeds, when she was just outside city limits."

Empty or not, Chelsea's stomach convulsed, making a mess all over the bedroom floor. Falling forward to her hands and knees and choking on her vomit, the only thing she could say was, "Damn you, Zech."

Zech snarled in response. "If I'm damned, you're damned with me! Thanks to you, I found out I'm not only good at killing, I *Like* it. And once I'm done with you, with everyone else's eyes on Cooper, there's no one left to stop me. No one who will even think loving, devoted Zech would have anything to do with this."

"What are you going to do to me?" Chelsea knew better than to ask, but it slipped out before she could stopherself. . Her whole world was spinning again, and her injured head only made it worse.

Once Chelsea was more stable, she heard Zech chuckling above her. "What I've been planning for a long, long time. But don't worry, I'll skip a few of my usual steps, you being family and all."

There was nowhere else for Chelsea to maneuver away, and she was no match for Zech. Knowing he could break her arm or dislocate a shoulder if he felt it necessary to gain the upper hand, Chelsea saved her strength for a later fight and let him tie her hands up and gag her. Getting a sock ball out of the nearby dresser wasn't hard for him, but where the tape came from was anyone's guess. He, too, had planned for this.

Shortly later, she was being mutely dragged towards the staircase, paralyzed with fear over the nightmares that were to come.

At the top of the stairs, Zech asked matter-of-factly, "Do you want to slide down the stairs yourself, or should I push you down?" Chelsea couldn't believe how casually he had asked her. He said it no differently than if he were asking if she wanted extra mashed potatoes during a family dinner.

Chelsea glared at him, but when Zech went to push her head first again, she crumpled a little and shook her head violently. The sock muffled her shriek, but they satisfied Zech's ears nonetheless.

Helping Chelsea lay down as comfortably as possible, Chelsea carefully slid to the bottom of the stairs and was barely sitting up when she was roughly grabbed and thrown to the floor. A second later, she saw what had caused such a reaction. Austin was standing on the other side of the iced glass door.

Not sure if he was her saving grace or her death sentence, Chelsea couldn't help but begin to hyperventilate. This was the first thing Zech had not planned for.

Threatening in a low, rough voice, Zech whispered, "You will not move, and you will *not* make a sound, or I'll start by removing your tongue. Got it!?" Dead was dead no matter what, but it was obvious Zech wanted to take his time with her, even at the risk of exposure. But Chelsea didn't want to lose her tongue, whether her death was swift or drawn out.

Chelsea barely nodded yes, and Zech crouched out of eyesight from Austin. It was appearant Zech was upset over the interruption, but he still carefully dragged Chelsea around the sofa, where they both knew she would be hidden if there was a need to open the door, and there they waited.

Austin didn't ring the doorbell. He didn't knock on the door. But there he was, pacing, torn between leaving or not. Agitated, Zech let out a little growl and got up. Chelsea couldn't see anything and could barely hear above the pounding of her own heart. Willing herself to calm down, she could finally hear their voices and tried to think of her next move.

Austin's voice was the first she could hear over the rushing in her ears. "… just doesn't feel right. And you know they investigated all of us. What we were doing was wrong."

"And that's why I don't want any of you coming over here for chats. I had no part in those extra house activities you all did, and I can't bring my family into this." Zech sounded so composed, so loving toward his family. It made Chelsea's stomach flip.

Austin's voice was not nearly as composed. "But that's it too. You can vouch for me, can't you? You know I didn't kill anyone. I couldn't! I'm not that kind of guy!"

"Yes, yes, Austin. I know you're not that kind of guy. And if anyone asks if you were involved in what they're accusing Cooper of, I promise I will come to your aid."

Austin let out of sigh of relief at Zech's offer. "You will?! Oh, thanks, man. I'm…I'm just so…I didn't think this was real. What that woman said about Cooper, and then the Feds show up. "

"What woman?" Zech's interruption was quick. Snappy. Austin stopped mid-sentence, taken aback by Zech's sudden change in demeanor.

Uh-oh, Chelsea thought. Zech was tracking her every move, that much he already said, but he would have never guessed Chelsea would reach out for help from one of his team. Up until now, he was her one and only accomplice. This changed everything.

"I don't know. She never said who she was. Just some undercover chick. But she knew a lot, man. I mean, A Lot. And-"

There was a brief pause before Zech snapped out, "What?!"

Chelsea could hear the cowering in Austin's voice."Well, she seemed to imply that Cooper was innocent. So, if she thought he was innocent, then why did the FBI arrest him? And why are you so mad? You're the only one who *didn't* do something wrong. Right?"

Silence followed. Chelsea could practically visualize the wheels tuning in Zech's head, thinking of how to make the unwanted man go away. But, like the rest of her afternoon, Zech did something she didn't expect. "Ozzy, you seem to have a lot on your mind. Come on in. I'll get us a drink, and we'll talk about all this." His offer was so genuine anyone would have fallen for it, and Austin was more than naïve.

Consenting with a sigh, Austin said, "Thanks, man. I could use one," before stepping inside and shutting the door behind himself.

Knowing what would happen, Chelsea, come what may, tried to do everything to keep Austin from coming too far into the house. She writhed and tried to make as much noise as possible, but she seemed to distract him instead of warning the man.

"What the hoof!" She heard him thump to the ground before she wiggled from behind the sofa and saw the 'Family' wood carving next to the man's crumpled form." Then she looked up. The monster hidden behind Zech's face was fully seen now. She knew she had crossed a line; he would soon make good on his threat.

Zech snarled out, "Now look what you've done!" She knew exactly what he meant. He had never killed a man, a friend, but that wasn't what angered him. He was upset about all the evidence Austin's presence was leaving behind.

Chapter 30

Chelsea loved soccer practices. At least, she did. But they take so long. She kept wishing that, at any moment, the family would walk through the door and stumble upon the crime scene, halting Zech in his place. But Chelsea knew her wish was doomed to be unfulfilled, and Zech was good at quickly thinking on his feet.

Going through Austin's pockets, Zech found his keys and pulled Austin's mid-size car into the garage. Chelsea was the first to go in. Her destination was the trunk. That would have turned out well for Chelsea, but Austin quickly joined her. Zech laid them facing each other in a most unflattering way. Then, a tarp was tucked over them, sealing out the light and any possibility of breaking a taillight or reaching any emergency pull valve. Austin's presence wasn't Chelsea's only hindrance, though.

Chelsea's shoulder was injured in her initial fall down the stairs, but after Austin was knocked unconscious, Zech unleashed some of his anger on her. Chelsea didn't think any of her ribs were more than bruised, but when Zech aimed a third kick, Chelsea had been balled up tightly, and his foot collided with her already injured shoulder. There was no mistaking that pain; her arm was splintered near the shoulder.

Chelsea's muffled shrieks of agony temporarily satiated Zech's rage as he dragged her writhing body by the injured arm to the car. Chelsea blacked out momentarily, allowing Zech to lift her limp body into the trunk. Knowing she would be further subdued, Zech laid Chelsea on her injured side.

Chelsea came to her senses just as Zech was bringing Austin to the garage. The jostling of the car as Austin's body fell heavily in the trunk brought more cries and tears to Chelsea's eyes, bringing a dark smile to Zech's face. Laughing before throwing the tarp over them, Chelsea realized Zech now knew any movement would bring unspoken pain to her. If Chelsea weren't already crying, she would have started then.

Chelsea wondered why Zech didn't get in the car immediately and drive off. The long pause between her trunk buddy being dumped and the vehicle starting was nerve-wracking. Then she remembered her mess in the bedroom and any downstairs cleaning needed, thanks to Austin's untimely interruption.

If her pain and fear hadn't blocked out all thoughts, Chelsea would have struggled and tried to break something, but maybe it was a good thing she didn't. Zech was already a deranged man, and just because he hadn't followed through with removing her tongue didn't mean it wasn't added to his to-do list. There was no need to make that list any longer.

Chelsea's thoughts finally turned to Austin. From what she could deduce, his hands were tied behind him, and there was still the tarp between him and the outside of the car. *Wow, Zech reallythinks things through.* It was both the highest compliment and the most terrifying realization.

Zech seemed to be extra jerky on the brakes as they drove through the residential roads, rocking Chelsea back and forth. The pain sent Chelsea into tossing waves of nausea, and for a second, she thought she would black out again. Chelsea prayed someone was a good neighbor and was spying on them, noting that something was amiss.

Chelsea thought and thought. That Zech was smart about his killings was a given, but how smart would he be in his hometown? Chelsea knew if he wanted to dispose of her in the same place he did Lindsey Tate, she had anywhere between twenty and forty minutes to come up with a way to save her and Austin's skin. Twenty and forty agonizing, stuffy, suffocating minutes would go by all too quickly.

The first thing she needed to do was wake up Austin. An adrenaline rush from the thought of a painful death did little to help her overcome the pain in her shoulder, so her sheer willpower to live and bring justice to Zech had to make up for it. The second thing she needed to do was get the gag out of her mouth.

If the sock in Chelsea's mouth wasn't muffling the noise so well, her painful cries would have woken Austin. Instead, Chelsea resorted to head-butting his chin repeatedly. In hindsight, she should have worked on the gag first.

Austin began squirming, which gave Chelsea a piece of mind. The hit sounded nasty, and his waking up sooner than later was a good thing. Now for the gag.

The sock ball shoved into Chelsea's mouth was initially a huge hindrance, drying her mouth and muffling any sounds, but now was the greatest help Zech could have given her. He had used duct tape to secure the gag to Chelsea's face, and experience told Chelsea all she needed to do was get the tape wet enough, and it would come off.

It wasn't hygienic, but Chelsea could do only one thing. Soaking the sock ball in as much saliva as she could muster, she began to bite down on the ball, pushing spit onto her lips and face. It was disgusting but effective.

It took a good five active minutes to work her lower jaw free, and Austin was more than conscious by then. Zech must not have planned for him to wake up so quickly because he didn't bother using noise-canceling maneuvers on the unexpected guest. And Austin was beginning to make a lot of noise.

Austin called into what he perceived was a dark void. "What?" or "Where am I?" and "What's going on?" were his phrases of choice. Austin didn't squirm around much, or he would have felt Chelsea next to him, and he was making too much noise to hear Chelsea's muffled responses until her gag was fully removed.

Chelsea was glad he was awake and making some noise, but Zech would gag him too if she didn't keep him from making too much. That would be the worst thing for them since, judging by the road noise, they were no longer in town but instead on the highway. Keeping Austin's consciousness a secret was the only chance they had to surprise Zech into making a mistake when he opened the trunk.

Working her hardest, Chelsea finally made the hole between the duct tape and her bottom lip large enough to push the sock through. Austin was already terrified, but Chelsea practically gave him a heart attack when she quietly said, "Austin, we need to get out of here."

"What the HELL!" That sent him squirming now, and a good jab to Chelsea caused her to bite down on her tongue hard enough to taste blood to stifle her cries.

Gasping for breath, Chelsea barely controlled her volume while she commanded, "Damn it, Austin, stop! Shut up!" Chelsea let out a few moans of pain after that, trying to stop herself from moving any more than she had to.

Austin whimpered, "Who are you? How do you know who I am?!"

Between deep breaths and escaped cries of pain, Chelsea tried to reassure the poor man. "It's me, Austin! The woman from the restaurant. Zech was the one all along, the killer, not

Cooper. And we have to get the hell out of here, or we're both dead!"

Austin surprisingly didn't move anymore. Going silent, Chelsea couldn't tell if he was in shock or had passed out from everything she just said. Thank goodness it was the first one because she didn't think she had it in her to headbutt him anymore with how much pain she was in.

"Zech? Zech did it?! And Zech has us? But… he's a good guy. He's –" Austin sounded like the pathetic man she remembered, but she needed him to step it up now.

"I know it sounds like a stretch, Austin, but you must believe me. Zech is the killer, I swear. And he *will* kill us once we're out of town, so we need to work fast. Now –"

The sound of screeching tires and twisting metal cut out her words. It's one thing to hear an accident from the side of the road or be in one as a buckled passenger, but it is entirely different from being in a high-speed accident while tied up in a trunk.

Chelsea blessedly passed out from the pain before the real damage to her body happened. If not, there was no telling what psychological damage could have been done. In the milliseconds before complete darkness, thoughts of Lexi, Miriam, the kids, Joe, and even Austin flashed before her eyes, and all she could think of was, "Oh no."

Chapter 31

How accurately the movies portrayed events in Chelsea's real life is eerie. The shoe-tie trick, bugging a house, the terrible stake-out diet… But waking up after a horrible accident was nothing like the movies. There was no gradual awakening to a Beep-Beep from a nearby monitor. The smell of sterilizer didn't assault her nostrils. Flowers didn't surround her in a bright room and she didn't have a caring nurse beside her willing to welcome her back to consciousness. Instead, it was a flood of remembrance, pain, and a haunting feeling of being surrounded by death.

Chelsea woke up with a start, and she jerked in the bed before the pain incapacitated her. She must have looked like hell because that's how she felt. Other than her arm, which was now in a cast, Chelsea felt like half her body was broken or damaged in some way.

"Hey, take it easy, Chels, I'm right here." The voice should have been a flood of relief but instead jolted Chelsea out of any thoughts that this might have been a dream. Every nerve in Chelsea's body was on high alert. Sounds were now too loud, color and light too vibrant, and everything that touched her felt like a crushing weight. Chelsea instantly began to hyperventilate and cry out, reflexively pulling at anything that felt restraining. The automatic pressure cuff would have been removed in under a second if her arm wasn't in a cast, holding her back.

Joe was up out of his corner chair and by her side before she could do anything to the IV lines and called for help from the nurses.

Immediately, Chelsea's room was flooded with medical personnel, but to Chelsea, they were only strangers who would do god-knows-what to her, and her response to them was feral. Alarms blaring in her ears and people calling out her name were the last things Chelsea heard, and Joe's face was the last thing Chelsea saw before once again fading into black nothingness.

The second time Chelsea woke up was closer to what one would expect. The hospital was careful to bring her back to consciousness as slowly as medically possible, and her senses began working again one by one.

Chelsea carefully turned her stiff neck toward a presence she felt was there before she could fully see or recognize who they were.

Joe was sitting by her bedside this time, holding her hand with one of his and slowly stroking her hand with the other while Chelsea came out of her mental fog. Not only was this to prevent Chelsea from reaching for her IVs again if she had another manic episode, but it was also one of the few places Chelsea was not injured.

As soon as Chelsea's eyes focused on Joe, tears began to stream down her face again. The tears quickly turned into sobs that Joe wasn't prepared to handle, so he stroked her hand and made shushing noises he assumed were comforting.

Her heart monitor spiked, but other than that, Chelsea was waking well. After her earlier performance, the lead physician warned the staff to stay away unless their presence was absolutely necessary.

The heart monitor continued to ring out, and Chelsea's breath began to come quickly again. Gripping Joe's hand in hers with her little strength, Chelsea's eyes pleaded for Joe to understand when all she could say was, "Zech. He, he!"

Trying not to make any sudden moves, Joe tried to get Chelsea to calm down again before the medical staff forced her to go back to sleep.

"Chelsea? Chelsea. It's okay, you're okay now. They have Zech. He will never hurt you or anyone else again." The words were calm and controlled in a way that belied Joe's true feelings. After reassuring her repeatedly, Chelsea could finally compose herself enough for the monitor to stop beeping.

Chelsea understood she was safe and Zech was gone, but other than that, Chelsea's mind was still a jumbled mess. Questions flooded her mind. Where was Zech? Austin? How badly was she hurt? Where was Lexi or Miriam? And when was she going to get her next dose of pain meds? But no matter how hard Chelsea tried, she couldn't focus on one question long enough to ask it.

Chelsea didn't have to wait long for her answers, though. Joe was never comfortable with silence, so he began to talk to fill this one.

"We probably have another half an hour before the nurse returns with your meds. They wouldn't tell me much about your injuries, but Miriam should be able to fill you in on everything they needed to do."

Chelsea finally looked at her body for the first time. Her initial assessment was correct; nearly half her body was covered with a bandage. Lord knew how her face looked, the way it was throbbing.

Chelsea let go of his hand for a second to feel her face. As she expected, a bandage was on her left eyebrow and chin. Her nose felt hurt as well, but she didn't want to touch it. Her hands felt like she was touching a deformed monster, breakingher heart.

"Miriam wanted to be here when you woke up, but…" Joe stopped abruptly. The uncertainty in his voice caught Chelsea's attention. Joe held on to Chelsea's hand again and cleared his throat. Chelsea stared at him for a few seconds before he continued, unable to look Chelsea in the eyes as he did.

"Zech survived the accident as well. Miriam is with him now, but he has extensive brain swelling. The doctors don't know if he will ever wake up."

Joe was unaware of Chelsea's silent tears until he felt the tremors in her hand. Joe was no stranger to helping victims of various crimes, and tears were no stranger to him, but Joe couldn't bring himself to see Chelsea in such a state. So, Joe remained looking away, rubbing the back of Chelsea's hand with his thumb in a way he meant to be comforting.

"Miriam wants to see you. The FBI is here too, so you can expect some company once everyone knows you're awake." Chelsea could only shake her head a little, the pain quickly putting an end to her movement.

"No," Chelsea's voice was hoarse, and her throat was dry and painful. She must have been on a ventilator at some point. "No, I don't want Miriam here. Not yet."

Joe noticed Chelsea looking at the clock and knew what she was thinking.

"Lexi is at school with Ethan and Kayla. She was here all yesterday. Everyone agreed the kids should continue life as normal as possible before everything goes public. God knows how everything will change then."

Chelsea's heart ached for her niece and nephew. It ached for Miriam, too, but something else was behind her feelings for her sister. Something she couldn't define yet. But Ethan and Kayla? They were the latest victims of their father's crime spree.

"Do you want me to pick Lexi up early?" Joe's question tore through Chelsea's thoughts.

Chelsea wouldn't have to worry about Lexi's initial reaction to her injuries, but that wouldn't make facing her daughter any less painful. Like her cousins, Lexi should enjoy her last day of normality.

Joe was finally looking at Chelsea, waiting for a response. Chelsea asked, "Are you sure they don't know? What happened and why?"

Joe shook his head, "All they know is you and Zech were in a car accident with another friend. But the news will get out sooner than later."

Joe mistook Chelsea's fresh stream of tears and stood. "I'll be right back with Lexi."

Chelsea said, "No, later." That surprised Joe. Trying to swallow, but only aggravating her throat more, Chelsea asked one more question. "Austin?"

Joe's pitying look sent the full weight of guilt slamming into her, blocking all the raw nerves and deep aches from her mind. Austin was only in that trunk because of her. He was only involved in this investigation because of her. He was only dead because of her.

"No," was choked out as she began to sob all over again. How could she live being responsible for yet another person's death? "What – his family. Joe, he was only there because of me!"

Joe wouldn't accept that reasoning. Getting as close to her without touching, lest he invoke even more pain upon his best friend, Joe made sure she held eye contact before going on. "Hey, Chelsea? Chelsea, you listen to me right now. You are *not* responsible for Austin's death. You didn't put him in that car, Zech did, you hear me? Don't shoulder the burden Zech put on you."

There was a flurry of activity outside her door just then. They were caught off guard when a nurse slipped into the room to get out of the way of the officers and medical staff surging down the hall. Seeing she was caught, the nurse walked over to them and tried to look like she was more on a routine check-up than getting caught hiding.

The nurse glanced at the whiteboard hanging on the wall. "So, Misses Markwell-""Miss," Joe pointedly interrupted for Chelsea.The nurse paused. "Excuse me?""Miss, not misses," said Joe rather forcefully. "And since you're not her usual nurse and not on her rotation, seeing as I checked everyone personally, please tell Nurse Ken that *Miss* Markwell has come out of her medical coma."

Chelsea couldn't see Joe's face, but his terse voice made his feeling unmistakable. The look on the nurse's face (would she call it shocked? Startled? Definitely out of sorts) was priceless. As Joe had requested, the woman quickly slipped away and searched for Nurse Ken.

"I guess I'll have to get Lexi and the others now anyway," Joe said this more to himself than Chelsea as the two of them watched a few news reporters walk by their room. "It seems your story leaked out earlier than anticipated."

When Joe turned back to her, she couldn't help but feel her lips tug up at the right corner. "You did a personal background check on *all* my medical staff?"

Joe scrunched his face slightly before saying, "All *might* have been a bit of an overstatement." This led Chelsea to give Joe a full smile before he continued, "But I checked out this Nurse Ken guy. And I would understand if you would prefer a female nurse instead after, well, after everything."

Everything that happened with Zech, Chelsea mentally filled in. Suddenly, Chelsea's eyes returned to the door and all the ruckus on the other side.

"I don't want to see any guys, if possible."

Joe looked uncomfortable at that statement.

"Joe, if you think I'll kick you out of my room, then *you're* the one with the head injury. I know you have a lot going on, and Haley probably needs you, but please, don't leave me."

Joe sat back down on her bedside and took her hand once again. "I'm not going anywhere."

That wasn't exactly true since Joe had to request a nurse change. Due to her extraordinary circumstances, the staff was happy to oblige.

The commotion earlier that sent the nurse into Chelsea's room was due to gang-related violence instead of Chelsea's story. It was a tragically common event in that part of town, but Chelsea was thankful the commotion had nothing to do with her.

With Joe gone, Chelsea was alone in her room for a few minutes. She sat and breathed. It was peaceful and lonely. The world went on around her without her. No one bothered to think about the goings-on at a hospital in Tulsa, Oklahoma. No one thought about the horrors, the trauma, the deliverance, or the new-found hope. But the stillness and silence and peace were all too short-lived.

Chapter 32

Miriam came to see Chelsea when she heard her sister was awake. It was hard to tell which of the two women was hurting the worst out of all of this. Miriam had no physical injuries, but the invisible ones cause the most damage. Miriam had given herself no rest, no peace once she heard what her husband Zech had been doing over the years.

Miriam cried over her sister, wishing to embrace her but knowing that would cause more damage than good.

Many tears replaced few words, and the sisters spent most of their time thanking God above or reassuring the other all would be alright. Most of the sister's interactions over the following few days were like that, but Miriam was in Chelsea's room less often than Joe or Lexi. Miriam had to split her time between Chelsea and Zech.

Miriam hated Zech for what he did, and a part of her hated Chelsea for what she had gotten herself into. But Miriam also loved them both deeply. It was that love that burdened Miriam the most.

Ethan and Kayla were allowed to see their father once while he slept in the Intensive Care Unit. Ignoring their questions about the police guarding his room, Miriam told the children it might be long before their father woke up or saw them again and wanted them to make peace over the situation. They did, and just in time.

Once the serial killings and arrest were made public, all hell broke loose. No one was prepared.

A police detail was placed outsideChelsea's room. The family was given a full week before the news leaked out, and once it did, Chelsea's hospital room became a sanctuary for Miriam and the three kids.

Chelsea didn't need to be a spy to see the haunted and hollow looks on the younger faces, nor the shellshock in Miriam's eyes.

Public hatred is known to drive families to cling to each other or fall apart, and it was still too early to tell which way this would go.

Although the masses were kept at bay and out of Chelsea's room, the gossip could not be contained. Chelsea uncovered some valuable information through long midnight hours and several "Have you heard?" without needing to ask Miriam or Joe.

Sifting through last night's chatter, Chelsea found out Zech was still in the ICU, and it was unknown if or when he would wake up from a coma. However, Zech would be transported to "The Mac," Oklahoma's State Penitentiary, if he became stable enough.

According to the early morning nurse who found a man in uniform distracting and was perpetually late with Chelsea's pain meds, Chelsea was "lucky" Austin was there to buffer her from some of the crash's impact. There were others in the crash who were brought to the hospital and didn't survive.

Chelsea felt anything but lucky.

Chelsea would always feel that lingering guilt of bringing Austin into her mission in the first place.

The name of the female agent from the airport was Dobson. Chelsea didn't need gossiping nurses to figure that out. Agent Dobson was in Chelsea's hospital room within 24 hours of her waking up. She and Chelsea became fairly acquainted over the following two weeks.

It was hard to tell what Agent Dobson was most upset about, that Chelsea was right about Cooper being innocent or that Chelsea pursued the case after explicitly being told not to and was badly injured over it. Either way, what little respect Chelsea had for Dobson was now gone. At least now, there was no point in telling Chelsea to stay out of her cases. Nothing in the world would make Chelsea go back to spying.

One day in the two weeks Chelsea was in the hospital, Joe didn't stop by. That was the day Chelsea learned what had bothered Joe so much when she arrived back in Tulsa. It was also the day of his wife Haley's funeral.

There were always medical complications where Haley was concerned, but when she developed a cough that led to pneumonia, it was too much for her body to handle. Now Chelsea understood why Joe was so out of sorts and how Chelsea's lack of interest in Joe's personal life had hurt him so much. It also explained why Joe could spend so much time at the hospital despite not being on her security detail.

Haley's funeral was ten days ago now. Joe still wore his ring. Chelsea still didn't know what to say, so nothing was said. Nothing had to be said. Sometimes, healing isn't found in words.

Unfortunately, healing for the Mullen and Markwell family looked so far away, and it certainly wouldn't be found inside their house. Not when the public turned on Miriam and the kids, a tragic reality for most families of wicked people. The Mullens practically fled their home once Zech's full identity was released to the public. Chelsea helped Miriam and the kids relocate to a small Tulsa suburb upon her discharge from the hospital. Chelsea and Lexi joined them soon afterward.

After many months of court appearances and testimonies, physical therapy, PTSD therapy, and grief counseling for all, the two sisters were left with a mountain of medical bills to pay and one house to sell.

They sold it at a terrible price, but it was time for them to leave Tulsa behind for good. It should have been hard, leaving everything they had ever known behind, but it wasn't.

Chelsea asked Joe to come with them, but he couldn't. "I know I'm the man you want, Chels, but…I'm not the man you love. Not really." Joe said all this while fidgeting with his wedding band, still on his finger.

The rejection hurt, but after a few weeks, Chelsea knew Joe was right, and she loved him all the more for it. Joe would always be a part of her life, even if he weren't right there. Theirs was a friendship that would last a lifetime but only remain a friendship.

In the end, Miriam and Chelsea found themselves sitting on the back porch of a North Carolina property, watching the kids play in the sand and waves. It is still a long road to recovery for all, but it is a road they will travel together.

Chelsea looked out at the clear, breezy day. She could fullyappreciate it after all she'd been through, and yet, after all she'd been through, she knew grief could strike at any second. It took a long time for her bones, joints, and soft tissue to heal, but she was nowhere near that far in emotional and mental healing. But days like this helped, and at this house, days like this were pretty regular. She had a cold drink in her hand, beading up with condensation on the glass. Miriam sat next to her on the balcony of a North Carolina beach house that Chelsea's long-built real estate empire afforded them. The three kids played on the beach together, free from the weight of what had transpired, at least for the moment. The waves of the ocean were at a steady, dull roar. The kind of white noise that relaxes your soul. There would still be a long and sometimes bumpy road on the recovery journey, but the sisters and cousins would be on it together.